LITTLE SISTER

ELANA GOMEL

Let the world know:
#IGotMyCLPBook!

Crystal Lake Publishing
www.CrystalLakePub.com

CRYSTAL LAKE PUBLISHING RECOMMENDATIONS

Of Men and Monsters by Tom Deady

The Pale White by Chad Lutzke

A Season in Hell by Kenneth W. Cain

Quiet Places: A Novella of Cosmic Folk Horror by Jasper Bark

The Final Reconciliation by Todd Keisling

Apocalyptic Montessa and Nuclear Lulu: A Tale of Atomic Love by Mercedes M. Yardley

Wind Chill by Patrick Rutigliano

Little Dead Red by Mercedes M. Yardley

WELCOME
TO ANOTHER

CRYSTAL LAKE PUBLISHING
CREATION

Join today at www.crystallakepub.com & www.patreon.com/CLP

WELCOME TO ANOTHER CRYSTAL LAKE PUBLISHING CREATION.

Thank you for supporting independent publishing and small presses. You rock, and hopefully you'll quickly realize why we've become one of the world's leading publishers of Dark Fiction and Horror. We have some of the world's best fans for a reason, and hopefully we'll be able to add you to that list really soon.

To follow us behind the scenes (while supporting independent publishing and our authors), be sure to join our interactive community of authors and readers on Patreon (https://www.patreon.com/CLP) for exclusive content. You can even subscribe to all our future releases. Otherwise drop by our website and online store (www.crystallakepub.com/). We'd love to have you.

Welcome to Crystal Lake Publishing—Tales from the Darkest Depths.

It has been ten years since the untimely death of my mother, Maya Kaganskaya, a writer, intellectual, and dissident. She fought monsters of totalitarianism her entire life. With love and everlasting memory, this book is dedicated to her.

THE LOST NOTEBOOK

THE DAY HER father was arrested, Svetlana lost her notebook.

The notebook was important because all the latest definitions were there, written down in her careful round script. She searched for it everywhere: under the roll-up top of her desk, where balls of blotting paper nested like spider eggs; at the bottom of her satchel where she discovered an ink-stained white ribbon; on the floor of the classroom, crawling between the rows of desks until she was chased away by old Aunt Sonya, the cleaner.

She could not find the notebook and went home downcast. She could always ask her best friend Tattie. But Tattie lived five streets away and the winter day was drawing to a close—the sky was like a dusty bowl filling with darkness. It was at night when the oborotni came out and prowled the streets. Though the Patrols of Light were there to protect the workers coming home from late shifts, children were strongly discouraged from venturing outside after dark. Even if, like Svetlana, they no longer considered themselves children.

A snowball hit her between the shoulder-blades

and cold wetness trickled down through a rent in her old coat. The boy had dived into the gaping mouth of a house but she had seen enough of his face to know him for Misha, one of her classmates, rather than something more sinister. Lazy, stupid, good-for-nothing! Well, if anybody was destined to be caught by an oboroten, it was him! Svetlana defiantly stuck out her tongue and hurried on. A heavy hand landed on her shoulder.

"Little sister," said a hoarse voice, and a cloud of warm tobacco smell enveloped her, "where is the nearest dorm?"

She looked up. The day had curdled into a purple twilight. Sparse snowflakes shivering in the frigid air landed on the soldier's shabby greatcoat. His face, under stubble and dirt, was haggard and thin. He looked barely older than her.

"You mean a Visitor's House?" she asked.

"Whatever you call it here. A place to kip."

"Over there," she pointed toward the city center where the dark windows of granite-clad towers frowned at the wide boulevards lined with bare black trees. Many of the towers were abandoned, infested by the Enemy who wove its cocoons in the stuffy dark. There they were hatching new generations of shape-shifting oborotni, of brutal kulaki or Fists, named so because their faces were giant clenched fists, of wily kosmopolity or Kosmops, whose beguiling squeaks grew louder as their stature diminished in their successive generations—the latest brood were the size of rats—and worst of all, krovososy, the crawling vampires whose human bodies had degenerated into a fat wormlike tube, tipped with a toothy snout.

Or perhaps these scary images were yesterday's news. Wasn't there something about a new menace: former people, the living dead? Svetlana once again bitterly regretted her inattention in class. She had written down today's definitions in a daze of fatigue, their meaning sliding off her mind like water off a duck's back. Of course, she was tired but this was no justification for slacking. She was not the only one to have spent the night glued to the dining-room mirror and listening to the Voice.

She had been mesmerized by the Voice's rich cadences, but most of all she had been entranced by the everyday miracle of His words materializing into tiny flame soldiers who marched off into the darkness to do battle with the Enemy. She loved watching this happen. How unfortunate that one paid for sleepless nights with drooping eyelids and a foggy head the next morning. Her parents had fallen asleep on the couch, still sitting upright, as if she would not notice.

Now, her notebook was lost and she was unprotected against the Enemy's inexhaustible wiles. What was it the teacher had said? In addition to the former people, mertvetzy, there seemed to be a new variety of the krovosos that walked upright and had a human face with a coiled proboscis hidden in its mouth, like the stinger of a bee. Or was it a new oboroten?

Svetlana realized that the soldier was looking at her expectantly. She blushed. So much for her good manners.

"I'm sorry," she said. "It's a ten-minute walk. I'm going in that direction. Would you like to come with me?"

"Sure."

As the soldier fell in step by her side, Svetlana became aware of the profound stillness of the city. The shuffling of pedestrians, the screech of streetcars, the smart marching of the Patrols, all had been hushed by the snowfall. The only sound was a soft rustle coming from the soldier's feet that were wrapped in layers of newspaper inside his scuffled military boots. The snow was now collecting on the ground, giving off a pale ghostly light.

"Are you on home leave?" she asked.

The soldier mumbled something.

"What?"

"I'm not . . . I don't . . . Shellshock, you know. Not very clear in the head."

Svetlana did not know what shellshock was but she nodded, afraid of appearing ignorant. Obviously, it was some new trick of the Enemy. It was hard to keep up with them. At unpredictable intervals, the Voice would issue from a mirror, illuminating the Enemy-infested darkness with his flaming words. Most of what he said was incomprehensible, though sometimes an occasional sentence or even a whole batch of them would sound quite ordinary, and she would tremble, suffused with love and gratitude for His guidance. But even if the entire speech were spoken in no human language, it did not matter, for His word was made light, and life, and battle. Then, there would be classes for schoolchildren and emergency meetings for adults, where the Voice's pronouncements were painstakingly translated into new definitions and instructions for rooting the Enemy out.

Svetlana wrenched her thoughts away from her lost

notebook, glanced at the soldier again. What if he was a Word incarnated? Often, as she watched flame soldiers disappear into the darkness, she tried to imagine them swell up to human size, clothe themselves with flesh, acquire names, faces, eyebrows, birthmarks, zits . . . Nobody knew whether it actually happened, but she liked to believe it did.

"What's your name?" she asked.

"Andrei. And yours?"

"Svetlana," she said a little reluctantly. Normally she was very proud of her name, which meant 'light', but she liked the way he called her 'Little sister'. This is how nurses were addressed, and Svetlana had decided long ago that she was going to be a nurse when she grew up, healing the devastation wrought by the Enemy on the human bodies and souls. Not everybody had to be a warrior, she told her classmates, and though some boys curled their lips in contempt, the teacher agreed.

"Svetlana? Sveta? I had a sister named Sveta."

"Really?" she smiled at him. "So, you can still call me 'little sister'."

The bent pin holding her hair under the kerchief chose this moment to break, and her plait tumbled down.

He gently tugged the thick fair rope of hair braided with a threadbare ribbon.

"My sister was a pest. I bet you're a good girl."

"I bet you pulled her hair all the time and this is why she was angry with you," Svetlana giggled.

A black shadow detached itself from the ruined building at the corner, ran screaming toward them, its ragged coat of loose skin flapping over its shapeless body, a piercing shriek coming from the hole in its fist-face, the thick head-fingers stretching toward them.

"Run," Svetlana screamed but the soldier stood petrified. The sour stench of the creature washed over her, old blood and rancid fat, and despite the waning light, she could see with painful clarity the juddering sack of its belly, filled to bursting with the larvae of its young coiling under the pale membrane.

She tried to drag him away, but the soldier stood staring at the Enemy, his mouth hanging open.

He was a soldier; she was a schoolgirl, dispensable. There was really no choice. She stepped in front of him, shielding him from the ravening creature.

Then, a powerful side-blow sent her sprawling into the snow and a deafening noise exploded in her ear.

Svetlana scrambled upright. The soldier was bending over the creature that lay on its back in a pool of black blood, its belly-sack split and the larvae squirming feebly, trying to crawl out. In one hand Andrei clutched a curved stick. A thin smoke was coming from its end.

"Don't," she screamed when she saw how close he was to the kulak and its offspring. "Back off! They'll jump on you!"

He turned around; his face was the color of the steely-gray sky.

"What . . . ? What is this?"

"It's a kulak. A Fist. A big one. They're getting uppity, and the weather is good for them too. So cold."

"A kulak?" he repeated uncomprehendingly. "What do you mean? There was a kulak in our village, Uncle Vassily, but he was exiled . . . Anyway, this is not a man!"

"Of course not. It's a kulak!"

The larvae were now spilling out of the rent in the creature's stomach like a clutch of bleached earthworms. It was really terrible how their shapes approximated humanity. Wrinkling her nose in disgust, Svetlana stomped on them.

"What the hell are you doing?" the soldier dragged her away. "Those are babies!"

"Babies? What are you, daft?"

Suddenly a horrible suspicion blossomed in her mind and she backed away from him.

"Who are you?" she whispered.

He saw the change in her face and lifted his hand. "Little sister . . ."

"Don't call me this," she screamed. "Patrol!"

But there were no Patrols and no passers-by. The city lay empty around them: ice, iron, and broken concrete.

"Listen, Sveta," he said slowly, "I don't know what's happening, and where I am, and who the hell this monster is . . . I was fighting, okay? Kurskaya Duga. The Battle of Kursk. The fritzes were coming at us like bats out of hell and we were hunkering down in the trenches and the Commissar was giving his pep talk and then . . . I don't remember. I thought I had a concussion and was given some R&R. I heard from mates that it happens—your memory is wiped clean, like, and then it comes back . . . But sure as I am my mother's son, I could not have forgotten something like that!"

Half of what he said made no sense but despite this, she was curiously reassured that he was no Enemy. He seemed too human, too lost. The bewildered blinking of his eyes telegraphed his honesty to her.

"Who are the fritzes?" she asked. "A new kind of Enemy?"

"New kind? They are the enemy! German fascists. Lackeys of imperialism. Bloody vampires."

She nodded.

"I thought so," she said. "I knew you were fighting them, but where is your torch?"

"My what?"

"How did you . . . ?" her words petered out.

She had seen no flash of light, such as given off by the sacred electric torches of the Patrols. They were the only infallible weapon against the Enemy. Ordinary fire did not work so well—even assuming that there was something to burn, which increasingly, was not the case.

"How did you kill it?"

"With my Nagant, how else? You were just in line of fire . . . Why the fuck did you step in front of me?"

The question stung badly. Svetlana turned around and walked into the rising wind that cut her cheeks like broken glass and justified her tears.

Andrei caught up with her and grasped her arm.

"I'm sorry," he said. "I've to watch my tongue, I know, but this is what you pick up in the trenches . . . You're a nice girl. But I just . . . I just don't understand. Am I dead?"

"No," she answered sulkily, "you would know if you were, and former people don't talk."

He sighed.

"All right. Is there anybody around who can explain the situation to me?"

She was going to direct him to the Speak-House but they had already passed the street where the turn-off was, and darkness was gathering behind them, a frigid wall of livid purple and black enlivened with fleeting shadows.

"Well . . . " she said uncertainly. "My Dad. He knows everything."

"Please!" Andrei grasped her hand. "Take me home. I know it's hard for civilians now, but I still have my ration. Tobacco, even some chocolate . . . I'll share!"

She was not doing it for food but she did not argue. They hurried through the inky dusk, hearing the mournful cry of a krovosos from a courtyard.

"A vampire," she explained. "You must be used to this if you're fighting them all the time."

"Germans are pigs but they don't squeal like this," he muttered.

Svetlana's parents were already home. She hid her face in her mother's warm bosom, for once not being ashamed of behaving like a baby. Andrei was standing patiently at the door while she tried to explain to her parents who he was. Her mother frowned but her father invited him in.

While they were drinking tea with the promised chocolate—crumbly, and chalky, and tasting like heaven—Andrei looked curiously at the smoky homemade candles that sent legions of dancing shadows into the corners.

"I only saw those when I was a child," he said, "I thought all cities have electricity now."

"We do," Svetlana's father replied. "All the Patrols are armed with electric torches."

"Despite the blackout?"

"What do you mean, blackout?" Svetlana's mother asked sharply. "How could we fight the enemy if there was a blackout?"

"But the raids . . . " Andrei started.

From the standing mirror on the dresser came the Voice. The paper flowers in a glazed ceramic vase, poppies and carnations that Svetlana had made in her crafts class, instantly burst into flame. A stream of power poured into the tiny apartment, filling it with a cataract of sound, echoing from the peeling walls and shabby furniture, sweeping over the four people like a mighty river. Svetlana stole a glance at her parents' bowed heads, but the moment was really too private to share with anybody, even them. Trembling, she watched the feeble candle-flames shatter into seeds of fire that sunk into the already pitted and scarred floorboards. From these black holes, miniature flame figurines crawled out and rushed toward the window, galloping over the four people in their eagerness, leaving scorched streaks on Svetlana's arms and shoulders. She felt no pain.

The Words joined with the other flaming hordes rising from the lit windows of human families—too few, in the city encroached upon by the Enemy, but still enough to fill the frozen air with the maelstrom of dancing stars. Then, the host or Words shaped itself into a whirlpool of fire, rose, and disappeared beyond the clouds.

"What was that?" asked the soldier hoarsely.

He was huddling at the table, his hands sliding off his ears where he had clamped them, wearing a pained expression on his face.

"I thought it was a broadcast . . . sounded like, you know who . . . But no, of course not, I couldn't make out a single word. How can you stand this bloody noise?"

"Who did you bring into our home?" screamed Svetlana's mother.

The door burst open.

Dark helmet-wearing figures crowded the doorway, their torches stabbing the dusty air. Svetlana backed away from Andrei, torn between the horror of having been taken in by the Enemy and the gratitude to the Patrol for having arrived in the nick of time.

"Comrades . . . " Andrei took a hesitant step forward.

Svetlana thought, dazed: This cannot be. He should shrivel and crawl into the corner confronted with the Light, shed his deceptive human masquerade, reveal himself for . . .

But she could not finish the thought because the Patrol, a bunch of tired, callow youths, their leather coats torn and filthy, paid him no attention. Their leader, whose red star-crowned helmet sat askew on his shaven head, shoved him aside and marched toward Svetlana's father. Before she could process what was happening, before she could take in her mother's thin wail, he kicked the man to the floor and the Patrol crowded around him, their torches trained upon the huddled mass.

Svetlana threw herself at them, cannoned into their tobacco-smelling wall, pushed them aside, rushed forward to lift her father—and was caught by rough hands, pinned between two swearing, angry, tired young men.

But she did not even struggle. She looked.

Looked as her father, the kindest, wisest of men, rolled himself into a ball like a hedgehog, his arms covering his face tightly, but not so tightly that she could not see the transformation taking place.

The familiar face was sloughing off, washed away by a thin stream of evil-smelling liquid, and another face was unfolding like a poisonous flower. The hooked snout with needle-sharp teeth, the tiny ruby-colored eyes set so close to each other that they looked like a single raw wound below the bulging bony forehead, the forked black tongue, ceaselessly licking bleeding lips . . . His hands were fleshless claws now, and his stooped back arched into an animal spine . . . An oboroten? Her father: a shape-shifter, a werewolf!

Everything went black before her eyes and from far away she heard voices, distant and unimportant.

"Where are you taking him, Comrades?"

"Where else?"

"Stay with the girl."

"Calm down, Mother. We're doing you a favor."

"They never see it until it's too late . . . "

She understood each word but they made no sense. Nothing did.

THE EYELESS

WHEN SHE CAME TO, sluggishly and reluctantly, she found herself lying on the family's shabby sofa. Andrei was sitting by her side. A sparse dawn bled through the window.

"Mama," she whispered.

"She went after them," he said. "I told her not to . . . It's not a good idea. But she would not listen."

Svetlana stared at him. His face looked dusty. She noticed, distantly, a half-healed scar on his cheek.

"They took my Dad, too," he was saying under his breath. "A month before the war started. They said he was a cosm . . . cosmop?"

"Kosmop," she said. "It's a kind of vermin."

"This is what they said. I can't even pronounce it."

"My father is innocent," Svetlana said dully. "It was not . . . it wasn't him. Somebody made a mistake. I need to go and talk to them. Now!"

She tried to get up but fell back onto the sofa again. Her head was spinning, blue spots rotating in her field of vision.

"Hey, hey," Andrei pushed her back.

"You need to eat, little sister," he said. "I'll boil water, make tea. You just rest."

Svetlana lay back and closed her eyes. In the kitchen, Andrei was banging pots and pans, looking for loose tea.

"In the tin," she yelled.

He came back into the living room, holding a battered tin, shaking his head in admiration.

"Real stuff," he said. "Real Chinese tea. Haven't smelled it since I was a kid."

"What's 'Chinese'?" Svetlana asked. She was not really interested but needed a diversion. Anything to make her forget that her father . . . No! She squeezed her eyes shut, willing it all to go away, willing to wake up and find herself back in yesterday when the world had made sense.

"Where does this come from?" he asked, lifting the tin decorated with a discolored picture of women in red skirts gathering tea.

"The South. Swamp Country. We used to trade with them before they went bad. Now, I'm not sure."

Andrei shook his head. A vertical frown cut his forehead, as if he was figuring something out.

"Dead," he said, speaking to himself. "A bullet through the head . . . Quick death. So quick I did not notice . . . So that fat priest was right! There is something after death."

"You are not dead," Svetlana said impatiently. "Come on, don't you think I would know a mertvetz, a former person, from a living man? We did an autopsy on one in class and I got an A. My teacher said that I should go on to the POP Institute after I finish school because I'm so good at sniffing out the Enemy, but I told her I wanted to be a nurse."

A wave of grief and disbelief, as palpable as a slap

in the face, drove the words back into her mouth. So good that she could not see that her own father was . . . No!

Svetlana collapsed on the sofa, wailing. The sound of her voice was shockingly loud in the hushed apartment and she raised it even more, forcing the air through her scratchy throat, as if the sheer volume of her inarticulate cry could force the universe to respond to her, to make everything right. But the universe was silent.

When her sobs died down, she saw Andrei put a steaming mug of strong black tea and a plate with a heel of rye bread smeared with a thick layer of butter on the table before her. She was too nauseous to eat, but she was touched by his efforts. Her father never prepared food; it was a woman's job. Mama took care of cooking when she came home from her factory shift. Svetlana helped occasionally but Mama was reluctant to let her into the kitchen, wanting her daughter to focus on her studies.

She drank obediently, wincing at the cloying sweetness—it tasted like he had dumped several tablespoons of sugar into the tea. Andrei sipped from her father's chipped mug.

"All right," he said, "so if I am not dead, where am I?"

"Loadstone Rock."

"Is it your city's name?"

"Yes."

"Sounds familiar," Andrei muttered, "but how the hell did I get here? Anyway, that's a factory town, right?"

"Of course."

"What are you making here?"

"Weapons," Svetlana said proudly. "Weapons of light. To fight the Enemy. To build the future."

Andrei was staring wistfully at the bread and she realized he had not made any snack for himself. She pushed the plate toward him.

"I'm not hungry."

"Little girls have to eat."

"I'm not little!" she fired back, her face reddening. "I'm fourteen. Three candles already."

"What does that mean?"

"You start with one candle when you are seven. Two when you are ten. Three—from thirteen to seventeen. And if you are really good, really dedicated to the fight, you join the Light Patrols after that. Girls, too."

Andrei nodded. The tension in his face was draining away as if he was beginning to make peace with the holes in his memory. Svetlana was glad. She had already decided that he could not be of the Enemy: he was too kind, too solid, too reassuring. In the world that was so crazily off-kilter, he seemed to be the one real thing remaining.

But perhaps he had been affected by the Enemy? This must be it. Damagers! Yes. Svetlana suddenly remembered one of the definitions in her lost notebook. The teacher had been talking about a new kind of the Enemy that had been spotted in the factory precinct. Called vrediteli or damagers, these were fat colonies of pallid worms that had the ability to imitate, albeit imperfectly, a human being. Stuffed into a business suit, their swarming heads covered by a wide-brimmed hat, they could pass for a manager or a supervisor as long as one did not look too closely. When they approached a vulnerable piece of machinery, they would fall apart and crawl all over the precious gear, sliming the bright metal, clogging the moving parts, and bringing production to a standstill. As opposed to most Enemy kinds that infiltrated the city from the Wastelands outside, damagers seemed to breed in the heart of Loadstone Rock, which made them all the more dangerous. There was some talk of their being able to cast a kind of glamour over the workers that made them sluggish and confused. What if Andrei had been exposed to something like this? The Patrol had not touched him; he was human, after all.

Then she remembered who the Patrol had actually taken away, and denial and incomprehension crashed over her once again.

Andrei was busy rearranging his beat-up backpack. He had taken out the curved black thing that he had used yesterday to kill the Fist and was lovingly polishing it with a piece of cloth. Its black oily sheen drew Svetlana's eyes. She had never seen anything like that but somehow it seemed like a counterpart to the electric torches of the Light Patrols: dark where theirs were radiant, but equally deadly against the Enemy. She reached out, gingerly touched the warm metal.

"Careful," Andrei's tone was sharp, but then he smiled apologetically. "No, sorry! Girls can shoot, too, I know. I heard of a sniper named Lyudmila at Stalingrad; she had more notches than most guys."

"Notches?"

"For dead fritzes."

Svetlana did not understand but somehow his admission that she could do whatever it was that he had done with this strange object spurred her into action. She swung her legs over the edge of the sofa and stood up.

"Come on." Andrei put his hand on her shoulder, gently pushing her back. "Where are you going?"

"Speak-House."

"Is this where they took your Dad?"

She was unable to say "yes", her face flaming with shame. Speak-House used to mean protection and reassurance. Now she would have to go there as a disgraced supplicant, tainted by association with the Enemy.

"Don't go," Andrei said. "It's useless. My mother and sister, they used to stand in line for hours. They never saw him. They brought food and gave it to the guards who ate it. And we starved."

"I must," Svetlana insisted. "There was a mistake. There must have been."

"Don't kid yourself. You saw."

She looked away.

"Mama is there," she said after a pause. "I have to bring her home."

Andrei was about to say something else when footsteps were heard outside and the front door rattled.

Svetlana rushed to the door and collided with something that felt like a steel bar. It took her a moment to realize it was Andrei's outstretched arm, corded with sinews and covered by the rough fabric that smelled of makhorka tobacco. His other arm whipped up, and his hand clapped against her mouth. She was as helpless to move as a mouse in a trap.

"Shhh."

A rain of blows fell onto the door. Svetlana's family lived in a two-room apartment on the ground floor of a four-story building. The front door opened straight into the living room. There was a short communal hall outside, and the building had a sturdy entrance door, but it was never locked, so whoever was outside could have walked in straight from the street. The only door in the entire building that was always kept bolted and locked was the one leading to the stairwell.

"Quiet," Andrei whispered again.

Svetlana redoubled her struggle. Her suspicions came flooding back. Perhaps it was Mama coming back and the soldier was trying to keep her away.

No, Mama would have a key, and a Patrol would just break through.

Another wave of blows. They were urgent but curiously uncoordinated, as if a whole bunch of people were hammering on the door simultaneously, oblivious of each other. Not a Patrol, then.

"Don't answer," Andrei hissed in her ear. "Enemies."

The idea that the Enemy would knock was ridiculous beyond words, but Svetlana had no time to respond. The door shuddered and popped off its hinges. The group of people crowding the entrance hall was smeared into a gray mass by the pale winter light. They heaved like a field of weeds, eager to burst through, but with so many trying to do it at the same time, they got in each other's way.

Andrei swore and let go of Svetlana as he fumbled for his fire-stick. She stood still, trying to assimilate what she was seeing.

***

This was no Enemy raid. The people who had just broken into her apartment were perfectly familiar. Even in the tangle of shadows that swarmed over them, she recognized the faces of their neighbors.

Uncle Dima, Dad's coworker who had often lingered in their kitchen over a stein of kvas until it was too late to go back home and he had to snore the night away on the floor in a nest of old blankets, much to the indignation of his wife, Aunt Xenia.

Aunt Sonya, the school's imperious cleaner.

A thin woman with a face like a hatchet that Svetlana had seen in the bakery, arguing with the salesman over a squashed jam bun.

Misha, her good-for-nothing schoolmate.

And . . . and Tattie, her best friend, her small fists clenched above her head as she surged into the room, colliding with the sharp angle of the dining table. The collision sent her sprawling, and the rest of them, rushing after her, tripped and tumbled into a pile of flailing limbs. It was so clownish that Svetlana could have laughed, believing it was all a weird communal performance put on for her entertainment. Except that she finally saw what caused these people to flounder, stumble, and fall like newborn kittens.

Kittens were blind because their eyes were covered by a film. The eyes of the people in the room were covered by spiky black splotches that spread over their faces like ink-stains on a piece of blotting paper.

Tattie crawled from under the heap of the adults and surged toward Svetlana who whimpered and backed away. Her friend's dark plaits bounced down her back, one of them unraveling as the blue ribbon that held it together came loose. The ribbon was familiar, and so was Tattie's white-aproned school uniform, creased as if she had slept in it. But with those horrible blots covering her upper face, she looked as alien as an Enemy. They seethed and squirmed as if they were alive: spiderish sea stars drinking away human eyes.

Andrei stepped forward, raising his Nagant.

"Back off," he yelled. "Freeze or I shoot!"

"Stop!" Svetlana cried, shaking off her paralysis. She had seen what the thing could do. No matter what had happened to her friends and neighbors, she did not want them blown to pieces. But it was too late.

Tattie's outstretched hands brushed Andrei's military tunic and hooked into the fabric. He pushed her away. Meanwhile, the hatchet-faced woman zoomed in on the sounds of struggle and blundered toward them, her splayed fingers tasting air like a colony of worms. The rest of them did not bother to get up. They just crawled toward the soldier.

The shot was deafening in the confined room. Tattie spun around like a top, her white apron blossoming with a red flower. She crashed to the floor and lay still.

It had no effect on the rest of the blind people who kept advancing. Uncle Dima creeped over the girl's body as if it were as insignificant as a speed bump. But the splotches on her face reacted by detaching themselves. Two sooty, spiky, star-shaped patches slipped off smoothly and disappeared into the massing shadows on the floor, leaving behind two deep black holes where Tatttie's hazel eyes had been.

Andrei kicked Uncle Dima's ribs, aiming his army-booted foot so unerringly that the crawling man was almost lifted off the ground and crashed into the hatchet-faced woman. The rest paused, disoriented. They seemed raw and unused to their blindness.

Andrei scooped Svetlana up in his arms, jumped over the squirming barricade of bodies, and ran to the door. A hand closed over his ankle, and he stomped on it. At the entrance, he dropped Svetlana and beat at his trouser leg where a black patch tried to attach itself. He tore it off and trampled it into slime.

They rushed through the hall and exited into the pale light of winter morning, the white sky as brittle as glass. Svetlana's breath steamed and her lungs seized with a brutal jab of cold. She only had her house dress on, her padded coat, cap and mittens remaining in the apartment.

But the cold was the least of her worries when she saw what was happening outside. Their street was swarming with people.

On a regular day, men and women would be walking to the factories, singing and laughing, exchanging jokes, eager to resume their work. Children would march through the streets in orderly columns on their way to school, waving flags of Light or, on special occasions, burning torches. A Patrol would show up occasionally and people would jostle and crowd to come closer to the stern-faced young men and women in their dusty overcoats and star-crowned helmets to yell their appreciation of their fight, and to press into their hands home-baked goodies and, in summer, flowers. Older people who stayed home to take care of babies too young for the crèche would also step out when the weather was good, to breeze in the atmosphere of good cheer and common will that pervaded the city of Loadstone Rock.

What was happening now looked like a nightmare version of such a regular day.

The people were a chaotic mass flooding the street like a military parade gone awry. They pushed and shoved. They shouted, but instead of uplifting slogans, what issued from their mouths was a stream of broken syllables, all the more terrifying because it occasionally coalesced into a meaningful denunciation of the Enemy. Their faces were blinkered with squirming black sea-stars, some tiny like an eye-patch, some so big that they covered everything but the screaming mouth. They were blind but they moved forward with the tenacity of migrating caterpillars.

Andrei whirled around but the flood of eyeless people was coming from both ends of the street. He looked up to where the apartment blocks jutted into the colorless sky.

"Up," he yelled in Svetlana's ear and pulled her back into the entryway of her building where the always-locked door to the stairwell loomed threateningly in the dusk.

He pushed the door, but it did not budge. The first eyeless scouts were now squeezing into the hall, colliding with, and momentarily hampered by, those who were crawling out of Svetlana's apartment. Andrei pulled out his Nagant but holstered it back. A shot would only reveal their location.

Shaking off her paralysis, Svetlana darted toward the stairwell door and groped under the filthy rug on the floor, through the accumulation of debris and dead cockroaches. Her fingers closed upon the chunky key.

She fumbled with the lock while Andrei kicked away the grasping hands. The eyeless were as strong as they had been before whatever had befallen them had wrought the horrible transformation. They were getting better at coordination, as if the shock was wearing off. Before the overwhelming human wave could drown them, the door swung open and Andrei and Svetlana dove in, slamming and locking it behind their backs.

THE SEALED FLOORS

THEY FOUND THEMSELVES in the dirty darkness, faintly diluted by the anemic light dribbling from an unshaded electric bulb. Svetlana was momentarily surprised by the fact that there was electricity in the sealed floors but then realized it was necessary to keep whatever was breeding here in check.

The light was so dim, though. Would it even work?

She looked around. She had not been to the upper floors since she was a child and remembered little of them. Ahead of them, a flight of concrete stairs disappeared into the gloom, littered with desiccated insects and mice droppings. There was a shed to the right where the janitor's tools used to be stored when the entire building had been occupied.

Andrei looked back at the door that shuddered but held as the fists of the eyeless hammered at it.

"Funny neighbors you have," he remarked acidly.

"Don't you dare." Svetlana turned on him, her cheeks blazing with indignation. "Those are good people. Good workers. The Enemy had done something to them."

"What?"

She shook her head mutely. She had never heard

of anything like this. A whole neighborhood turned into . . . whatever. There were no words in her vocabulary to describe something like this. There were traitors, of course, occasional people seduced by the Enemy and gradually mutating into monsters, but so many and so sudden?

Then she realized what it meant, and relief washed through her, momentarily blotting out fear and confusion.

If ordinary people could be so beleaguered by the Enemy as to become crawling ghouls, then what had happened to Dad was just another unmerited affliction. He had not willingly sold himself to the shape-shifters, walking corpses, screaming fists, and wormy damagers. He was not a traitor but a victim. Surely, the Patrolmen and the officials in the Speak-House were right now working on how to reverse the plague. Svetlana could not wait to get to the House where she could talk to whoever was in charge and explain the situation, and make sure Dad was cured. And bring him home.

She turned to Andrei, glowing. He was looking up the staircase. Suddenly, she remembered the red flower on Tattie's chest, and her exuberance faded.

"Is there an attic here?" Andrei asked. "Can we get to the roof?"

Svetlana caught his sleeve.

"Don't go up," she exclaimed. "The house is infested. The Enemy has taken over the apartments here. This is why they sealed the upper floors."

Andrei shrugged.

"It's either that or the bunch outside. There are too many to shoot our way through. You learn it a hard way, little sister: when it's one against a thousand, the one loses. We have to try our luck on the roof."

He started climbing. Svetlana stood still. What if she could just wait it out? Surely the eyeless would eventually go away.

The door shuddered under a new barrage of blows. Andrei rounded the corner of the staircase, disappearing into the gloom, and Svetlana could not bear parting from him. She started climbing, almost tripping and falling in her haste. As she groped her way in the murk, clinging to the slick banister, she tried to convince herself she was only doing what was right by looking out for him. He was a warrior; his life was precious.

The bulb on the next landing was on as well, and Svetlana's spirits rose. If there was electricity here, then the Patrols must have left it on deliberately to protect the ground floor where her family lived. Light was watching over them, after all. They were not alone.

But the electric lamps were so weak that they only generated small puddles of yellowish glow. The air in the stairwell was stagnant and smelled rusty and rotten at the same time. Something crunched wetly under Svetlana's slippers.

They reached the next floor.

There were two apartment doors on the opposite sides of the landing. Dark red with recessed panels, they looked like the door of Svetlana's family's apartment except for being gouged with deep scratches. Both were firmly closed.

As they stepped onto the landing, the door on the left swung open. Clotted darkness swirled inside.

Svetlana gulped and hurried on to the next flight

of stairs, but Andrei peered into the apartment, and then he dived into the darkness.

"No," Svetlana cried, poised above the landing. The stairs ahead of her were blocked by something long and thin lying across them.

At least she could hear Andrei who was blundering inside the apartment, swearing and rattling something in the gloom. Svetlana forced herself to step down.

The electric bulb on the landing exploded, showering her with slivers of glass. The dark was as palpable as a dirty hand clapped against her face. A wave of stench rose toward her—gangrenous flesh and blocked latrines.

"Andrei," she cried.

"Here!"

She fumbled forward, hands outstretched, horribly reminded of the eyeless people's groping fingers. She brushed her face to make sure no writhing sea-stars blocked her eyes.

She homed in on the sound of Andrei's voice. He was swearing incessantly. Something crashed. Then another noise—an insidious rustling.

"What the . . . ?"

In their own apartment there had been electricity once, before all the production had to be diverted to the war against the Enemy and its foreign sponsors. All the apartments in this block had the same layout. If she could just keep her cool, pretend she was in her own familiar living room where she could find her way blindfolded . . .

Svetlana's hand touched a hanging cord, furry with dust. She tugged.

The ceiling fixture turned on.

The light was weak but shed enough illumination for her to see the cluttered room, Andrei in the corner, and the thing rearing above him.

It looked like a giant pale snake, but its flesh was soft and lardy. Its head bore a tiny human face perched askew above its proboscis like a coquettish hat, and it had rudimentary arms, pudgy and useless. They were waving in the air as the thing dipped toward Andrei, its proboscis swelling and growing.

The electric light upset the krovosos and it hissed as Andrei ducked, snatched up a chair and hit the creature that writhed on the floor, its pulpy body flailing around like a giant leech. After the third blow, it exploded with a wet crunch, red blood spraying out and splattering the walls.

***

Tossing the splintered chair away, Andrei came over to her, wiping blood splatters off his face.

"I thought you did not have electricity indoors," he said.

"We used to. I knew where the switch would be. But why did you go in?"

Instead of an answer, Andrei turned to a big oak wardrobe with elaborately carved doors. Svetlana's family had never had anything so grand. Was this the reason the people who had lived here had been vulnerable to the Enemy? Everybody knew that hoarding was one way to let Darkness in.

Andrei rooted inside the wardrobe and pulled out a heap of musty-smelling clothes.

"It's winter outside, little sister," he said.

Svetlana had to admit he was right. Her flowery housedress would be useless in the biting cold, and Andrei's greatcoat had been left behind as well.

They pawed through the clothes. Andrei took a worn overcoat patched up with random pieces of leather and fur. It had been owned long and lovingly, and Svetlana looked queasily to the corner where the smashed body of the krovosos lay like a human-sized blood sausage. Had the master of the house been masquerading as a man until exposed by a Patrol? Or worse: had he not known what he was?

"That's for you," Andrei said, handing her a woman's cable-knitted jumper, so big it fell to her knees. It stunk of old sweat but she was relieved there had been no children in the apartment as all the clothes were adult size. She supplemented the jumper with several scarves.

Dressed as warmly as possible, they went back out onto the landing. The long thin thing that Svetlana had seen on the stairs was still there, as immobile as a log.

Perhaps it was a log . . . but then the thing stirred and slithered down the stairs. It looked like a slimmer version of the krovosos but Svetlana saw, just in time, that instead of a leech-like proboscis crowned with a cartoonish human face, it had a bunch of pointed serpentine heads that thrashed and squirmed in the dank air.

"Hydra," she hissed into Andrei's ear. "Stand still."

She pressed into the wall, hoping the creature would overlook them. Immature hydras were notoriously stupid, but once grown to a full size, they were more dangerous than just about any other kind of the Enemy. Hydras could not be killed except by fire. Cutting off their heads only multiplied them indefinitely.

The creature flowed by them and disappeared into

the open doorway. Svetlana and Andrei rushed up the stairs.

Another landing. Yet another. The building was old, as few constructions in Loadstone Rock were, and its massive stairs, substantial doors, and carved banisters exuded the air of unclean antiquity. Not for the first time, Svetlana wished they had been given one of the smaller but newer apartments in the factory blocks. Perhaps then what had happened to Dad would not have happened.

She almost collided with Andrei when he stopped abruptly, pointing at something hanging from the sloping ceiling of the stairwell. She looked up.

They were cocoons, almost ready to hatch. One of them split on top and a small pink hand was poking through the oozing slit. There had been kids in the upper floors, after all.

On the next landing, there were no apartments but only a small postern door in the corner. They went through and found a narrow staircase leading to the attic. The door was not locked but unfortunately it meant that there was no way to lock it behind them either.

The attic was huge and freezing cold. There was a hole in the roof and tiny dispirited snowflakes drifted through.

The attic was cluttered with old plywood boxes, moth-eaten rags, bundles of old clothes—detritus of interrupted and destroyed lives. Somehow these pitiful remnants of the everyday brought back the horror of the Enemy more vividly than the monstrous encounters in the sealed floors below.

Svetlana peered through a skylight in the slope of

the roof. The sun was invisible, and the sky was that peculiar lemony-gray color that presages winter twilight. But the golden lights of the Speak-House shone brightly in the dusk. They must have spent longer in the sealed floors than she realized.

She pointed out Speak-House to Andrei: a massive concrete block, its multiple windows aglow, and the squat tower above lit up by spotlights.

"That's where the Central Committee sits?" he asked.

"We call it the Council of Light, but yes."

"And the NKVD . . . I mean, like, security organs?"

"The Patrol of Patrols. POP."

"Do you really want to go there?" Andrei asked.

Svetlana did not deign to reply.

Andrei rubbed the dirty glass. "There is a walkway to the next building," he said, pointing.

From below, came the bang of a door.

They climbed the ladder in the corner and exited through a hatch, finding themselves on the icy shingles of the roof, which sloped toward a dizzying drop to the pavement four stories below. Once a parapet decorated the edge, but time and neglect had taken their toll, and now only gape-toothed remnants of the low wall stuck out here and there.

Something large passed over their heads. Svetlana followed the blackbird's passage until it disappeared behind rooftops. Blackbirds, piloted by brave Patrolmen, were a recent glorious invention of the Voice to ensure Motherland's victory in the coming war. Seldom seen, they were a thing of wonder, and under different circumstances, Svetlana would be mesmerized by the slim tubular body and large flapping wings feathered with silver. Now, though, they had more pressing concerns, like how to escape this infested building.

Andrei walked to the very edge, balancing on the slippery surface. Svetlana swallowed as she peered down to the pavement. She reminded herself that a nurse on the battlefield was supposed to be as brave as any soldier—braver, because soldiers' lives depended on her. She pushed down her fear and followed, clinging to fat chimney-pots for support.

Andrei looked down into the street:

"They are gone, the eyeless ones," he said.

"But the Enemy would be out in force," she pointed out. "We should wait till morning to go to the Speak-House."

"Not here."

As if to lend support to his words, a bouquet of wormy heads bloomed out of the hatch.

"Come on," Andrei yelled and, grasping Svetlana's hand, pulled her to the walkway that connected her building to the next one. The problem, though, was that the other building was lower, so the walkway was basically an openwork slide, without any railings and glassy with frost.

Svetlana took a tiny step. Then another.

She saw a fat pigeon flap through the air below her.

She stopped. Her knees locked.

"Move," Andrei yelled. "Move, you fucking coward!"

The insult landed like a slap in the face. Her eyes brimming with tears, Svetlana walked on. She did not see where she stepped, and it did not matter. Who cared whether she lived or died?

Andrei caught her in his arms. They stood on a shaky fire-escape attached to the brick wall of the next building. There was a smashed glass door leading inside.

The building, too, was abandoned. Fortunately, it had never had families living in it. Consisting of dusty corridors and empty offices, it had probably served as a neighborhood distribution center. Sparse electric lights were on.

They found shelter in a small office with lots of moldy paperwork still lying around. Andrei collected old files and posters and made a fire in a potbelly stove. Normally Svetlana would object to this willful destruction of official documents, but she felt exhausted, dispirited, and empty.

They huddled by the stove. Andrei lit up a rolled cigarette.

"I'm sorry, Sveta," he said awkwardly. "Mama would paddle my behind for using this kind of language on a girl. But you learn bad things in the trenches. I won't do it again, I promise."

Svetlana nodded without looking at him.

Her stomach rumbled and her eyes smarted with unshed tears. Eventually, she fell asleep.

THE SPEAK HOUSE

THE STREETS WERE empty the next morning as they trudged through the shivery frostbite of the crystal air toward the Speak-House. Svetlana was so cold that even her thoughts seemed frozen in her head. She clung to one certainty—she needed to talk to the people in charge and tell them what she had seen. Hopefully, then her parents would be restored to her, and everything would be as it used to be.

But what about Andrei? He marched by her side, his face set in a frown. He was her witness. If her story of the eyeless was doubted, he could lend his support. Would he be believed? Wouldn't he be suspected of being in the service of the Enemy? How could she know for sure that he was not? Okay, he could not be an Enemy himself; something deep inside her insisted on his humanity, but what if he was a foreign infiltrator of some kind?

When they had woken up in the office, she had been unable to move, her limbs seized with the paralysis of chill. The fire had gone out in the night and the windows were painted with rime. When Andrei pulled on his boots, the newspapers he used to pad them crackled like frozen autumn leaves. He tossed them aside. Svetlana picked one up. A large headline blared at her: "Victory in Operation Kutuzov!" Another one: "How many Hitlerites did you Kill?" Still another: "Under the Leadership of Comrade Stalin . . . " She could not understand it. It was in her own language and yet made no sense. She was about to confront Andrei when he picked up the newspapers and shoved them into the stove where he had managed to light another fire. At the time she had been grateful for the feeble gust of warmth; now she questioned whether he had done it to prevent her from asking questions.

Svetlana bit her lip. Her rational mind insisted she should be suspicious of this man with his strange weapons and stranger words. At the same time, she trusted him as much as she trusted herself, but she did not know why. Paradoxically, this increased her self-doubt. Could one be of the Enemy without knowing it? Schoolbooks said nothing about such anomalies.

They had not eaten for twenty-four hours. Andrei asked about canteens. They had one in each neighborhood, of course, but Svetlana was determined not to listen to her stomach as the urgency of her parents' situation drove her to the Speak-House.

"They'll feed us," she said.

On the other hand, what if they were too busy with the eyeless to listen to her?

As they walked, she saw that normalcy was grudgingly reasserting itself. A straggling line of workers passed by, their faces drooping but not disfigured by black patches. They looked at Svetlana suspiciously and she had to resist the impulse to tell them she was not playing hooky from school.

A Patrol barreled down the street without paying them any attention.

They passed a canteen. The door swung open and they were enveloped in a cloud of steam smelling of cabbage pies and buckwheat porridge. Svetlana's mouth filled with saliva. She would have resisted the temptation, she told herself, but Andrei stepped in and she followed.

Inside, a plump woman in a stained apron was stirring a large pot on the counter. Several people sat on the benches at the trestle tables, but the morning rush was over. Some glanced at Svetlana and Andrei with dull curiosity. Everybody seemed tired and out of sorts this morning.

Belatedly, Svetlana realized that she had left her ration card in the apartment, but Andrei confidently pulled out a worn wallet with documents and showed it to the plump woman. Svetlana caught a glimpse of the logo that included a strange curved symbol alongside a familiar red star.

"Sergeant Andrei Kurchenko of the 50th Army, 17th Rifle Division," he said smartly. "Here for some R&R."

The woman did not even look at the paperwork. Her face was the color of putty, fat cheeks sagging.

"We don't accept those here," she said. "Only the new cards issued by the House."

Andrei's face flushed dangerously:

"I'm killing fritzes on your behalf, mother," he bellowed. "Defending the home front! And you are telling me I can't have a bowl of soup?"

Svetlana stepped forward to defuse the situation.

"He is a soldier," she said. "Fighting the Enemy. We

are on our way to the House! But we are hungry. I . . . I lost my card . . . we had a commotion yesterday . . . ”

She trailed off, unsure how to describe yesterday's nightmare. The woman turned away.

“Get a new card,” she said indifferently, “and come back.”

“What new card?” Svetlana cried in frustration. “What are you talking about?”

She turned to the people on the benches.

“Comrades,” she appealed to them. “Maybe you don't know me but my parents are workers in the munition factory. This man has just come back from defending our borders. He is a soldier! How can you deny food to a soldier?”

The choking sensation in her throat warned her she would burst out in tears and she stopped, unwilling to be seen as a hysterical little girl. One of the men on the benches got up. He looked like a human basset hound with hanging jowls and puppy-sad eyes.

“Come on, Tamara,” he addressed the fat woman, “give them some chow. On my card.”

Tamara shook her head.

“You know I can't do it,” she said in the same monotonous voice. “I'll be arrested, and you'll be too. The Patrols are out in the streets with orders to check everybody's papers. Let them go to the House and get new ration cards, and then they can come back here.”

The basset-hound man shrugged helplessly, as if to say, “I tried.”

Svetlana turned to him. “Thank you, Comrade,” she said politely. “Can you please show me your new ration card, so we'll know what to ask for?”

The basset-hound man pulled it out from the pocket of his oil-stained overcoat. At first sight, it looked no different from the cards Svetlana and her family used to have—the man's name, number and blurry picture, surmounted by the symbols of the Motherland: the electric torch, the loudspeaker, and the red star.

Except the star was no longer red.

Instead of the familiar five-pointed symbol, the upper right corner of his laminated card bore a sooty design that looked like a tiny sea-star with spiky arms. It was slightly bulging, standing off the laminated cardboard, and as Svetlana looked, it seemed to twitch.

She quickly thrust the card back at the man and pulled Andrei out of the canteen.

***

They stood in front of the Speak-House, feeling as tiny as a couple of mice lost in a granary. The House dwarfed them as it dwarfed every visitor. It was a ten-story concrete behemoth, as wide as a city block, with rows of tiny square windows. Its central section was crowned by a fat tower with an electric star on top. Its beaten-bronze doors, decorated with a stylized design of beaming torches held by muscular hands, were easily as tall as a two-story building. Normally there would be two Patrolmen standing ceremonial guard by the doors. Today there was none.

Svetlana swallowed and stole a glance at Andrei who stared at the House, his face unreadable. She had only been inside once with a school tour. The grandeur of the building made her problems feel shameful and insignificant.

Mama was there. Dad was there—sick, perhaps,

but he was her Dad nevertheless. And the solution to the eyeless epidemic was there. She marched forward, shivering in her crusty layers of castoffs, and touched the door handle.

The giant loudspeaker mounted above the door suddenly cleared its metallic throat.

"Comrades!" the loudspeaker announced in a pleasant masculine voice. "Stand by for an important announcement from the Council of Light."

The loudspeaker was the reason for the House's name. Svetlana knew that what was being said here and now was simultaneously broadcast in every school, factory, plant, and canteen in the city. Her schoolmates would be standing in assembly now, drinking in every word. She would give everything to be there again, surrounded by her friends, to return to the untroubled days when a lost notebook was the greatest of her worries.

Then she remembered Tattie's blind face and the red flower on her chest and realized nothing was going to be the same again.

"Comrades!" the voice continued. "A new conspiracy of the Enemy has been unmasked by our heroic Patrol of Patrols. Those inhuman monsters managed to pollute with their stinking touch the sacred symbol of our struggle: the red star. POP has discovered that the red stars on your ration cards and other official documents have become a source of contagion, afflicting our innocent citizens and robbing them of their eyesight. Please come to the Speak-House as soon as possible to turn in your old documents and receive new ones. Our brave Patrolmen and women will pass through the city and remove and replace signs and slogans affected by the Enemy's despicable wiles. We shall overcome this setback, as we have overcome all the others. Under the guidance of the Voice and with our eyes firmly set on Light, we shall triumph over the Enemy!"

A wave of canned applause and cheering washed over Svetlana and Andrei. She pushed the door, which moved easily, and they stepped into the House's giant foyer.

The foyer was flooded with bright electric light. After the winter dimness outside, Svetlana was blinded. Blinking away tears, she looked around.

The blaze was generated by the electric sconces affixed to the marble columns that marched around the foyer. There were banners and slogans, rippling sheets of rainbow-colored fabric hanging from the domed ceiling far above their heads. There were several enormous pedestal-mounted loudspeakers. After a moment, she realized that though the foyer was quite big, it was not actually as huge as it had first appeared. The illusion of size was produced by the fact that the back wall was a mirror, doubling the bright space and reflecting their hesitant, ragged figures on the threshold.

There was a small desk, as incongruous as a toy. Sitting behind it was a stout, uniformed woman with permed gray hair, busily sorting through a stack of ration cards.

"Dear Comrade," Svetlana approached her. "Could you please direct us to a representative of Patrol of Patrols? We have an urgent matter to discuss."

The woman looked up at Svetlana who gasped and backed off. The woman's eyes were in their proper places in her lined face but instead of pupils and irises, black spiderish stars twitched in the discolored whites.

The woman cleared her throat.

"Your cards," she rasped. "Give them to me. Need to be exchanged."

Svetlana was paralyzed with shock, but Andrei quickly grabbed her arm and pulled her away.

"This place is infested," he whispered. "Traitors. Let's go."

"Cards," The woman repeated shrilly.

A group of uniformed Patrolmen appeared on top of the wide marble stairs leading to the upper floors where Council offices and POP headquarters were located. They looked familiar and reassuring in their long leather overcoats and peaked star-decorated helmets, but a second glance confirmed Svetlana's worst fears: their eyes squirmed with black spiders and the stars on their helmets were spiky and black instead of red.

"Halt!" their leader yelled as Svetlana and Andrei retreated toward the entrance doors. The Patrolmen pulled out their electric torches, and their beams, dazzling even in the brightness of the foyer, converged on the two. Svetlana automatically stopped. Electricity killed the Enemy, but everybody knew that it was harmless and even beneficial to true citizens. Perhaps now they would see that she was no Enemy spawn, that her father had been the victim of a terrible mistake . . .

Instead of caressing her with a touch of Light, the beams stabbed her like red-hot knives. Her layered clothes started smoking and a welt formed on her cheek where a beam glanced off.

"Run," Andrei yelled.

Svetlana stood frozen, unable to overcome her disbelief that this was happening. Those were Patrols of Light who had protected her since she was a babe in her mother's arms. Running away from them was like running away from herself.

The beams whipped at Andrei and his greatcoat caught fire. He shook it off and tossed it at the Patrolmen.

"Run! These are fritzes, fascists!"

The Patrolmen moved down the stairs and the black stars on their caps writhed as if alive. A thunderous crack deafened Svetlana and she saw one of the Patrolmen fall. Andrei gripped her arm, almost wrenching it out of the socket, and dragged her back into the street. Wrapped up in a cocoon of shock—even her father's arrest had not been as traumatic as discovering the rot of treason in the Speak-House— Svetlana mutely followed him through the swirling snow that had started falling while they had been inside. She felt as if she were floating. Andrei was swearing as monotonously as a stuck gramophone, but Svetlana could not understand what he was saying. Her parents had been very strict about protecting her from the bad language spoken by shirkers, lazybones, and other anti-social elements.

"Where to?" Andrei hissed in her ear.

This did rouse her. She suddenly realized that he was the only thing left to her—this stranger whom she had met less than two days ago. She was not afraid of dying but losing him was intolerable.

She looked around and pulled him into the grated entryway of a courtyard. The oatmeal-colored veils of snow billowed out as indistinct figures rushed past them down the street. The snowfall obligingly erased their footprints.

There were no children playing in the courtyard as there would be on a regular day. The skeletal swings and the lopsided slide were covered with white snow-sheets as if in preparation for a move. This could be because the school was still in—or for a more sinister reason. Svetlana owned no timepiece, of course. Only Council officials did, but normally there was no need as loudspeakers blurted out news on the hour and there were large public clocks on all main intersections. But she had not heard any loudspeakers for quite some time and had forgotten to look at the clocks. Would she trust them in any case? In a world gone mad, what if time itself had been corrupted?

She no longer felt cold and she knew how dangerous that was. The whispering caress of the snowfall could lull them into death.

Taking Andrei by the hand, she led him through a succession of courtyards, linked to each other by dank passages smelling of urine and mice. Kids were told not to use those, but most did anyway. Gossip about girls snatched up by krovososy only added to the piquancy of disobedience. Svetlana wondered dully why she had ever thought that danger was exciting.

Andrei was still gripping his strange weapon that he called the Nagant but eventually holstered it when it became clear they were not being pursued.

"Running out of ammunition," he muttered.

They came out of the labyrinth of courtyards close to Svetlana's house. Through the thickening veils of gently falling snow, she could see that the street was empty.

Fearfully, she searched for Tattie's body in the drifts but there was no sign a girl had been killed here.

Andrei took off his cap and put it on Svetlana's head. Only then did she register that she must have lost her scarf somewhere and that wet clumps of snow were accumulating on top of her head, soaking her braid, and dripping cold moisture down her unprotected neck. The cap, too big for her, only added to her discomfort by sliding off and blocking her vision.

But this was what Mama or Dad would have done. Tears streamed down Svetlana's face, but she no longer sobbed aloud—the world was quiet, white, and deadly, and in the snow-hush even the sound of crying could be their death sentence.

Andrei tugged her braid:

"There, there, little sister," he whispered. "I won't leave you, I promise."

THE TRAIN STATION

THEY HAD GONE back to Svetlana's apartment because they could think of no other place to go.

The door was sealed with a black spider-star, but Andrei unceremoniously kicked it in. It was freezing inside because the central heating had been turned off. It was routinely done when an entire apartment block had to be written off as a nest of the Enemy.

Otherwise, her family's possessions had been left untouched. There was food in the larder, and the kitchen stove still worked. They made giant mugs of tea and ate bread and sausage, huddling under heaps of blankets.

Svetlana had lived in this apartment since the day she was born. Her textbooks still lay in an untidy heap on the desk in the corner of the living room that doubled as a dining table when her parents were on different shifts and the family did not eat together. The paper flowers she had made, scorched by the power of the Voice, drooped in the vase made of a jam jar. She could see into the kitchen where the family's mismatched plates were displayed on the open shelves and the big table proudly bore the white cloth her mother had embroidered with a cross-stitch pattern.

A fat-bellied kettle on the stove breathed out a thin ribbon of steam. The mirror from which the Voice issued was decorated with red cloth streamers that she used to wash by hand, reverently, on each laundry day. It was home. But it did not feel like home anymore. She saw shabby, cramped, sad rooms filled with worn-out furniture and knickknacks. She saw water stains on the walls. She saw a dim bulb in a dusty glass shade failing to dispel the clotted gloom of a winter day. She almost saw through the flimsy jousts and peeling plaster of the ceiling to the monsters breeding in the sealed floors. How could she have ever thought she was safe here?

The feeling of revulsion toward her family home came with a dollop of shame at her own treachery but also with a powerful wash of relief. It made what she had to do easier.

Andrei was deep in thought, staring into his mug as if it was an oracle. Svetlana surreptitiously studied him from under her lowered lashes. She realized that she had never gotten a good look at him. They had been either running or planning where to run next. There had never been time. He was a stranger.

Yet, he did not feel like one. She had never seen him until he called her "little sister" in the purple twilight, but somehow, he looked as familiar as if she had known him her entire life. Could they actually be related? The population of Loadstone Rock was knitted together by a complicated web of kinship—cousins, second cousins, uncles and aunts several times removed—so it was not impossible. But they did not look alike. Svetlana had large blue eyes and fine straight hair, so blond that it was almost white—a source of her private anguish as she inwardly compared her "straw" to Tattie's dark, bouncing curls. Andrei's skin was tanned and weathered, his hair black and his eyebrows looked like silken cords. Black stubble was showing on his chin. Despite this, he did not look much older than herself. Svetlana pegged his age as eighteen but only because this was the age of military draft.

He finally put the mug aside and cleared his throat. He seemed ill at ease, his eyes sliding off her face. She was also jittery, trying to steel herself for what she was about to say and casting about for the right words.

Andrei spoke first.

"Listen. Sveta . . . " he said slowly, still avoiding looking at her. "I'm sorry but I . . . I need to go back. To my buddies. To my battalion. I hate leaving you but I . . . I don't belong here. I don't know what it is we are fighting. For my country. I can't . . . can't leave them. I can't desert. Deserters are traitors. I won't be a traitor."

So much for not leaving me, she wanted to say but bit back her words, recognizing that he was right. Treachery to Motherland was the one unforgivable sin; loyalty to Motherland was the one supreme virtue. A promise given to an individual counted for nothing compared to that.

"I understand," she said carefully. "Of course, you must keep on fighting. You are a soldier. Fighting the Enemy is what you do. But we are going together."

Andrei started.

"What? No way! Kurskaya Duga is no place for little girls!"

Svetlana was so offended that she overlooked the incomprehensible place name.

"I am not a little girl," she said haughtily. "I am going to be a nurse. Nurses go on the battlefield. But first I must go tell the authorities what's going on here. The Enemy has penetrated the Speak-House and POP. They are killing innocent citizens. They have taken my parents. The Voice needs to know!"

Andrei stared at her with a strange expression, almost as if he recognized something in her he had not seen before.

"And how are you going to do it?" he asked.

"I am going to the City of Light. I am going to speak to the Voice. You are coming with me as my witness. This is more important than beating back another Wulfstan incursion. This is our fight now."

***

After half-an-hour of back and forth, they decided on a compromise. They would go to the train station together. Andrei was rather hazy as to where he was supposed to go from there, and no wonder. The place he had named did not exist. Svetlana knew the geography of Motherland perfectly well, and no boundary town where skirmishes with foreign invaders were taking place bore any resemblance to whatever duga which was a ridiculous appellation anyway as "duga" meant "arc". Svetlana was convinced that he would eventually shed his delusions and follow her to the City of Light.

The main station of Loadstone Rock was close enough to her apartment to be seen from the living room window. It was a large handsome old building, painted yellow, with a clock-tower and a waiting hall lined with benches where passengers in transit would nap until their train chugged to the platform. Svetlana pointed it to Andrei, and they started packing. A train ride to the City of Light could take hours or days, depending on the route.

At least they could retrieve their own clothes, shedding the tainted rags reeking of the Enemy. Svetlana breathed in relief when she put on her own fur-lined boots, a down parka with a fur collar and a woolen headscarf. Andrei found his warm greatcoat and his fur hat. They filled their rucksacks with bread and sausage and walked out into a swirl of white.

Snow fell in large fluffy flakes, seemingly materializing out of the mauve air. Svetlana relaxed a little. This kind of snow always calmed her down, bringing with it magic dreams of distant lands and exciting adventures. They walked in easy silence through the hushed twilight world, but the magic spell was broken as they got closer to the train station.

The first indicator of something being wrong was a woman stumbling toward them. She was big and dressed in a voluminous fur coat, but the coat was unbuttoned and flapped around her as if trying to escape. She slipped and fell into a snowdrift but instead of trying to get up she just remained there, face down, her shaggy sleeves spread out like wings.

Svetlana rushed toward the woman, but Andrei restrained her and approached carefully, turning the woman over with the tip of his boot. She was not dead as Svetlana had feared: she flopped feebly, churning up handfuls of wet snow and shaping them into accidental snowballs. Her eyes were missing.

She looked like Tattie when the girl had collapsed, felled with Andrei's fire-stick, with two gaping holes in her blood-slicked face. There were no spiky stars, though. Either the woman had managed to tear them away or they had left her.

"Aunt." Svetlana knelt by her in the snow. "What happened? Can I help you?"

The woman, giving no sign that she had heard, flapped like a gutted fish. A wave of commotion coming from the direction of the train station broke through the curtain of snow. More people ran pell-mell past Andrei and Svetlana and disappeared down the street. They were so quick that she could not be sure whether they had eyes or not. Andrei peered into the white confusion, while Svetlana tried to help the woman up. It was like trying to lift a flour-sack.

"Leave her," Andrei yelled. "She's gone."

Svetlana was outraged. This was not how the People of Light were supposed to treat each other.

A new sound joined the cacophony of shouting, coming from behind them: a staccato rattling as if somebody was throwing handfuls of dry peas onto the pavement. It was accompanied by a high-pitched hissing.

"Kosmops," Svetlana yelled.

Kosmops were the most insidious kind of the Enemy. They existed in three distinct generational forms. Starting with something that was human-sized and human-shaped—enough to deceive a casual observer—they quickly bred into dog-sized snarling predators who just as quickly whelped a legion of humanoid rats. The third, smallest generation was the most dangerous. They fouled grain supplies, gnawed through water pipes, and would often bring down an unwary child or kill a baby in the cradle. And then the cycle would begin anew.

Leaving the woman in the snow—she had finally subsided into an immobile hump—they ran toward the station. They almost collided with a solid wall of people who blocked the wrought-iron gate which normally would be unbolted and guarded by a Patrolman with a torch. Now the gate was half-closed and a bunch of people inside the station were apparently trying to close it completely, while the people outside were just as determined to keep it open and to push through. Shouts and curses filled the air. The pristine snow was being trampled into a filthy slush that sent some people flying off their feet. Children were crying, women wailing. From behind Svetlana and Andrei came the unmistakable rattle and hiss of the approaching kosmops horde.

Trains were the foundation of the regime of Light, its trusty mechanical soldiers that could never be corrupted by the wiles of the Enemy. Railway tracks linked all the corners of Motherland, spreading over her vast body like a web of arteries, carrying life-giving supplies: food, iron ore, wood, stone, and people.

When Grandma Olga was still alive, she would take baby Svetlana to the station to watch departing trains or would walk along the tracks as far as the outskirts of Loadstone Rock, following the bracing smell of hot metal and the soothing chug of locomotives. When the unclean noises of the Enemy at night kept her awake, Svetlana would strain to hear a plaintive train-whistle and fall asleep, knowing that Light was unconquerable. Seeing the station in chaos was almost as bad as seeing her father arrested.

Andrei, on the other hand, perked up, as if the fog of bewilderment that had wrapped him from the moment of their meeting suddenly dissipated. Squaring his shoulders, he made a path through the dense mass of people, yelling on top of his voice, "Let me through, Comrades! Important! Army business!"

Svetlana followed through the channel he cleared in the crush of bodies like an icebreaker cutting through an ice pack, wondering at people's gullibility. Who did they think he was?

For that matter, who did she think he was?

The interior of the station was engulfed in a melee. If there were any announcements made by the loudspeakers, they could not be heard above the screaming and shouting. The air smelled of garlic and dirty clothes. The waiting hall was creepily dim—the electric lights were off, and the only illumination was of the winter afternoon trickling through the skylights in the roof.

Andrei, with the assurance of long practice, maneuvered toward the swinging doors leading to the platforms, but they were guarded by a line of Patrolmen who shoved back the human flood with curses and blows. Svetlana could not see their faces under the peaked helmets. Wasn't this unbecoming behavior proof that they had also been infected?

Pushing through the crowd was like trying to wade through a river in flood. A jab of an elbow made Svetlana double over in pain. The people who manhandled her as if she were a piece of abandoned luggage were ordinary citizens: their eyes were clear of black stars, but maddened by fear, they were no better than the Enemy. The horror of discovering how fragile the forces of Light actually were, inside and outside the human heart, made her sluggish and stupid.

Fortunately, Andrei seemed to be in his element. Quickly appraising the situation, he pulled Svetlana to the side. Around the hall, benches had been pushed to the walls and piled up with burlap sacks. They jumped onto the sacks and circumnavigated the hall, kicking away grasping hands and thrusting shoulders.

As they approached the line of Patrolmen, they could glimpse the platform through the swinging doors. A train stood there, its cars hung with clusters of people like human grapes. They were pushing and shoving to get inside and were being met with the equal counterforce of the passengers crowding the gangways and the ladders and pushing them out.

The situation was mysterious, Svetlana thought. Why were some people allowed to board the train while others were barred? She did not have much time to ponder this question as the human sea at the entrance to the hall heaved, and the gate was torn off the hinges by the irresistible momentum of the mob. It seemed the hall was already so packed that no more people could get inside, yet somehow, they did. The stampede was gathering force, mowing down the people already inside like an avalanche. Svetlana saw an older man stumble and fall. He was instantly buried under trampling feet. The screaming rose as if somebody turned up the volume on an invisible loudspeaker. No matter how pumped up with despair, it could not drown the dry rattling and shrill hissing coming from the outside.

Andrei squeezed her arm, the two of them balancing on the sack that shifted under their feet, its contents—probably beans or peas—rolling around. The Patrolmen at the entrance to the platforms were pushed out like the cork from a bottle of champagne. The crowd spilled onto the platform, pursued by the knot of creatures that entered the hall.

Svetlana's mouth went dry. All three forms of Kosmops were present. Towering above the rest were tall humanlike figures wrapped up in their signature black trench-coats that were part of their hide. She knew that you could tell Kosmops from humans if you came closer, but in the dimness, they looked like well-fed Council bureaucrats from the Speak-House. Their retinue, however, instantly gave them away. Milling around their feet were snarling, slavering creatures that looked like bald dogs with oversized jaws and pink crania. The rattling came from them. Their tails were like those of rattlesnakes: flat, bare and with a series of hardened scales at the end. The intolerable high-pitched hissing was emitted by the swarm of the smallest form—two-legged rats whose fleshy puckered lips vibrated with the sound.

The massacre that ensued only imprinted itself on Svetlana's brain in strobe-like images. The bald dogs sinking their teeth into people's throats, blood fountaining black as the scant light dripping through the glass curdled to dusk. The two-legged rats leaping around, biting and scratching, two of them worrying at a baby plucked from its mother's arms. The trench-skinned creatures fanning through the crowd, dragging away kicking and screaming girls. But the thing that she would never forget as long as she lived was that the Patrolmen, all of them holding electric torches, lowered them and stood aside, watching the slaughter and letting it happen. Even as Andrei was dragging her to the platform, she looked back, hoping to see a dazzling beam cut through the chaos of slaughter, but there was no Light.

Then, they were on the platform, running toward the train which suddenly stirred like a waking cat and emitted a soft purr that quickly grew into a rhythmic chugging. The wheels below its metallic skirts shuddered and kicked into action. A shrill whistle, promising travel and excitement, drowned the noise of people being killed.

Andrei caught a ladder just as the train was beginning to move. The ladder and the gangway between the cars were so packed with people that Svetlana wondered dully whether it would be possible to squeeze in two more. She felt strangely remote from what was happening, suspended somewhere beside her own body like an observer. She realized that she was in shock, the events of the last days catching up with her, but she could not summon the energy to care.

"I'm a soldier," Andrei bellowed. "Going to the frontline! She is a nurse! Make room, Comrades!"

At the same time, he worked his elbows and knees, corkscrewing through the human mass. Miraculously, it worked. Where there seemed to be no free space even to drop a pin, a gap appeared. Squeezing and pushing, dragging Svetlana through the ranks of fuggy bodies, Andrei made his way into the car.

Its interior was a sea of people. This was apparently a long-haul train, so there were sleeping berths in small cabins, but their doors had been taken off to make more room. Each berth, meant for one, held at least three people squeezed together, the feet of those in the upper berths dangling in the faces of those below. The corridor running alongside the cabins was covered with old newspapers and entire families camped up there, sharing food and yelling at those who tried to make their way toward the far end where a flimsy partition hid the toilet bucket. Its stench added to the stifling bouquet of cigarette smoke, sweat, and fear that fogged up the car. Even though it was freezing outside, Svetlana immediately started sweating in the heat of so many bodies.

Andrei homed in on one of the upper berths. It was already occupied by two thin-faced lookalike women, but his stern demeanor must have frightened the twins because they mutely slid aside, folding themselves together like a fan. He pulled Svetlana up and they wedged themselves into the tiny space that looked like luxury to those on the floor, judging by the envious glances and muttered curses flung in their direction. Normally, Svetlana would be embarrassed by this lawless show of force—she was no better than anybody else and there should be an orderly queue, some authority to organize the people—but she was too tired to care. As the train lurched forward and the car swayed rhythmically, she hid her face in Andrei's scratchy overcoat and fell asleep.

COMRADE KRASNOV

SHE WOKE UP when the rocking of the train suddenly stopped. Muzzily, she lifted her head, marveling at the empty space around her. Then, she realized she had almost half the berth to herself because Andrei was gone.

She was instantly alert, her heart hammering. The people below murmured uneasily. The twins on her berth still huddled together, keeping as far away from her as possible. The naked bulb above swayed in the smoky air but at least electricity gave some protection against the Enemy who might be hiding in the mass of the passengers.

"Where are we?" she asked the twins, but they did not respond. They merely stared at her as if she had spoken in a foreign language.

Where was Andrei? Had he left while she was sleeping? Svetlana bit her lip, torn between relief and consternation. Since their twilight meeting, her life had been a string of disasters, and she still was not sure of who he was. Not one of the Enemy, this was certain, but her previous explanation that he was a soldier who had lost his memory due to battlefield trauma did not hold water either. First, he showed no sign of having been wounded. Second, there remained the enigma of his strange weapon, his unfamiliar uniform, and those weird newspapers he had had in his boots.

What if he was a foreigner? Motherland was surrounded by the iron ring of enemy countries, populated by inhuman monsters or humans who had willingly abandoned Light and sold themselves to Darkness. The Enemy was just a vanguard of those evil forces, ceaselessly plotting against the People of Light and their Voice. There was Thunderland whose inhabitants engaged in constant barbaric warfare, half-naked men clubbing each other with spiked maces, their women raped, and their children starving. There was the Swamp Country where the humans were enslaved by the devious Leech-masters: fat bags of lard with sucker-covered underbellies and smirking faces who minted gold out of their duped subjects' blood. There was the rotten Freehold where invisible parasites infested men's brains, causing them to shun Light. There were nameless little countries ruled over by kosmops and fists. Worse of all, there was the realm of Wulfstan where the Enemy had taken a human form. It was believed that the population of Wulfstan had, by now, been reshaped into the race of implacable bloodthirsty automata with baying canine maws and steel-clawed hands. Fortunately, the Voice, in his infinite wisdom, had negotiated a peace treaty with this dangerous foe, which gave Motherland a breathing space to strengthen its defenses.

But could Andrei be a native of any of those damned countries? Svetlana could not believe it. He was one of the People of Light. She had no real proof of it, but she felt it in every cell of her body. He may have called her "little sister" just to be polite, but now there was a bond of kinship between them.

Could he be a spy? Svetlana shivered because this was a much more real possibility. Denunciation of spies and saboteurs was a frequent part of the Voice's pronouncements. Spies were not necessarily of the Enemy; sometimes they did not even know who they truly were until the spell of Darkness had penetrated deep into their bodies and souls . . . Svetlana's mind shied away from the memory of her father like a finger refusing to probe an inflamed wound.

Her thoughts were interrupted when the mass of people below swayed and shifted like a field of corn as somebody was pushing through. Andrei! Oblivious to the indignant muttering in the wake of his passage, he elbowed aside a plump woman who squatted on her bags like a bird on the nest and jumped up into the berth.

"Where have you been?" Svetlana whispered.

Andrei blushed and nodded in the direction of the makeshift toilet. Svetlana smiled, pleased with his refinement—clearly, he was not of those kulak-breeding country people who took care of their needs in the open like animals. This was just one more proof that he was a person of Light.

Still, it reminded her of her own bladder. As solid as the plug of people below seemed to be, she would soon have to brave it. Perhaps some passengers would disembark at the next station.

Then she realized that since her waking up the train had not moved.

"Did you see where we are?"

"A small station. In the middle of nowhere. I could not see the name."

This was worrisome. Was the train even going to the City of Light? What if it terminated in some obscure provincial town or worse, a village? The countryside was infested with the Enemy. This was why so many Patrolmen were sent there to hunt down the Fists and to procure grain needed to feed factory towns. Recently POP had ratcheted up its efforts to arrest infiltrators from the countryside who came to Loadstone Rock to steal food. And there were those proscribed zones, the Wastelands . . .

Still, since nobody was disembarking, it must mean that this was not the final destination. Svetlana was trying to psych herself up to make her way to the toilet bucket when a wave went over the people below, heads turning in unison toward the sliding door at the end which suddenly flew open. A portly figure in the Train Service green uniform stood there.

"Tickets!" the man bellowed.

Svetlana and Andrei exchanged glances. Tickets had been the last thing on their minds as they were escaping from the spider-eyed Patrolmen and the murderous kosmops. Indeed, they could not have gotten tickets even if they had tried. Svetlana's minor's card did not allow her traveling beyond the municipal borders of Loadstone Rock.

Apparently, they were not alone in this predicament. A hubbub of voices erupted from the crowd.

"Tickets!" The conductor's roar rose to an almost supernatural volume, instantly silencing everybody. "Out everybody! Show me your ticket when you go by.

If I stamp it, go to the right. You'll be allowed to come back on the train. If not, go left! Now! Move!"

To emphasize that he meant business, two more uniformed figures appeared at the door, both cradling large military-style electric torches.

People started filing out obediently. Some tried to carry their luggage with them, but the big conductor barked an order to leave everything behind. Soon the car that had seemed to bulge with people deflated into an empty space littered with bags, sacks, and suitcases.

Andrei, Svetlana, and the twin sisters did not stir. They were on an upper berth, close to the shadows-veiled ceiling and perhaps they would go unnoticed . . . This hope was swiftly wrecked as the conductor, accompanied by the two Patrolmen, went down the car, checking out every berth.

Exchanging glances, they both jumped down and stood in front of the conductor. The twins remained in the berth, cowering and pressing themselves into the corner, as if hoping to become invisible.

"Tickets," the conductor commanded.

From close up, Svetlana could see his eyes. She breathed a sigh of relief.

Bloodshot and hung with dark pouches, they were, nevertheless, free of the spider-star taint, and the two Patrolmen had clear eyes as well.

"Who are you?" the conductor frowned, suspiciously eyeing Andrei's unfamiliar uniform. Svetlana opened her mouth, but Andrei forestalled her, which was just as well. It would be strange to have a young girl answer instead of a soldier.

"We are escaping Loadstone Rock where there has been a suspicious infestation," he responded smartly.

The conductor gave a braying laugh.

"You and everybody else on the train," he said mockingly. "Names? Cards?"

Svetlana offered her ration card which she had taken from her family's apartment. The conductor barely glanced at it.

"A minor!" he barked. "You?"

Andrei unhesitatingly offered him his strange documents.

"What is this?"

"These are my papers," Andrei said levelly. "They are real. Paid for in blood."

The conductor's sagging cheeks wobbled as he opened his mouth, then closed it, and motioned to Andrei and Svetlana to stand aside. The two Patrolmen hefted their torches but did nothing else as the conductor turned his attention to the twin sisters, still huddling in the berth.

"Down," he yelled.

They obeyed. Now Svetlana saw how frail they both were. It seemed that a gust of wind could blow them away. They stood up unsteadily, holding on to each other for support.

The conductor smirked.

"Fists," he declared. "Running away to the city, thinking we won't find you! Take them away!"

A Patrolman grabbed one of the sister's arms and hauled her out. The other followed as if glued to her twin. Svetlana was perplexed: were they really kulaks? They looked human, albeit unnaturally weak and emaciated.

"Valya!" one of them wailed, clinging to her sister.

"Valya!" the second one responded, like an echo.

They couldn't be both named Valentina, could they? But Svetlana had no time to puzzle over it because the conductor turned his attention back to them.

"Come." The conductor pushed Andrei and Svetlana out. The platform was filled with people divided into two uneven groups. The lucky ones whose papers were found to be valid were being herded back into the cars, while the illegals were being led away by a couple of torch-armed teenagers who seemed too young for such a task.

"Let POP decide what to do with you," the conductor muttered.

Despite being warmly dressed, Svetlana shivered. The sky was as white and flat as a blank page; steely snowflakes occasionally drifted down onto the dirty drifts that surrounded the platform. The snow must have thawed and frozen repeatedly because it was covered with a gray pitted crust, and a bundle of discarded clothing was embedded in it.

A Patrolman, hefting his chrome-plated torch, pushed them toward the exit from the station. As they passed by, the clothing bundle stirred and tried to sit up. A skull-like face emerged from the wrappings like a turtle from its shell. The hollow eyes stared through Svetlana. Then, the man settled back softly into the snow as if it were a down mattress.

The Patrolman yelled at them to move on, and they trudged down the icy track that led to a huddle of thatch-roofed low buildings. On both sides of the road, featureless snowfields stretched as far as the eye could see.

"What's the name of this village, brother?" Andrei asked.

The Patrolman spat makhorka-brown spittle. "Little Wells," he answered.

So, this was a village? Svetlana wrinkled her nose. Everybody knew that villages contributed to the defense of Motherland by feeding the cities where the sacred work of manufacturing weapons of Light was being carried on. But Svetlana was a city girl and had no precise image of the countryside beyond the golden sheaves of corn on the cover of her textbook. What she was seeing bore little resemblance to the picture.

The track became the main street. Mean houses frowned at them with their shuttered windows. Bare trees stuck out of the snow, their black arms adorned with white sleeves. There seemed to be nobody around, not even a dog or a cat.

The bigger house they approached had a large banner above the entrance, frozen into a brittle sheet. But even under the furring of rime, the red star stood out. Svetlana breathed a sigh of relief.

Inside, a fat little stove radiated heat. A man sat at the table, going through reams of paper.

"Comrade Krasnov," the Patrolman saluted him. "Two suspicious elements removed from the train."

The man lifted his head. He was young, barely older than Andrei. His face was darker than his blond hair as if a summer tan still clung to it in the midst of winter. His blue eyes, ringed by the circles of fatigue, lingered on Svetlana. She blushed and hated herself for that.

Before the man even opened his mouth, Andrei stepped forward and launched into a detailed recital of all that had happened to them since their twilight meeting that had seemed to Svetlana to be lost in history but, in fact, had only happened three days ago. Krasnov listened attentively and without interruption. When Andrei described the arrest of Svetlana's father, Krasnov glanced at her again. She forced herself to return his gaze. She had nothing to be ashamed of, after all.

"I see," Krasnov said thoughtfully at the end. He had a pleasant baritone and spoke crisply, like an educated man, without the sloppy vowels of recent arrivals from the countryside that were mocked in Loadstone Rock. "So, you are not related, are you?"

"Not that I know of," Andrei said.

Krasnov lifted an eyebrow.

Svetlana, no longer able to contain herself, barged in, "Comrade Patrolman," she exclaimed. "Loadstone Rock, our glorious city, has been taken over by the Enemy. My Dad . . . he is a victim. So is my Mama. They are holding her hostage! You need to do something!"

Krasnov smiled, his face relaxing momentarily and then settled again into a frown.

"Normally, I would arrest you for spreading false rumors," he said, "but unfortunately I know you are right. We had info on this infestation already, but now I am more interested in the two of you. You said you came from the frontline on R&R," this to Andrei. "But where are you fighting? We have a peace treaty with Wulfstan."

Andrei snorted.

"I am fighting Nazis," he said and when Krasnov continued to stare at him, he shrugged.

"I think I come from a different planet, maybe," he said. "I read a book once . . . about the revolution on Mars. Is this Mars?"

"I don't know what Mars is," Krasnov said. "Are you saying you lost your memory?"

"More like I have a different memory. This," he swept his arm around, "is almost familiar but not really. Still, I know what you are doing, and I want to help. Maybe we are just fighting the same thing under different names."

Krasnov studied Andrei's passbook and then put it aside.

"I am not sure what this is," he said, "but the headquarters will figure it out. I don't think you are of the Enemy. Vadim," he nodded at the Patrolman who had brought them in, "says you are not afraid of Light. You were sitting under an electric bulb on the train."

"20-watt," Andrei mumbled, "not much. We have better ones at home."

Svetlana elbowed him indignantly, but Krasnov let it slide.

"We have a situation here," he continued. "Fists are breeding like lice. We have fulfilled our grain quotas, so you'd think they would leave Little Wells alone, but no. The more they starve, the more uppity they become. Now people are coming from Loadstone Rock—refugees, kids—and we have nowhere to put them up. We have tried to inform the City, but the lines of communication are down."

"Sabotage?" Svetlana breathed out.

Krasnov nodded. "Damagers," he said grimly. "We had not had their kind before. Now they are here, and the Fists are working with them, naturally. We are short on manpower. You," he nodded at Andrei, "you say you are a soldier. We are doing a sweep in an hour. Want to come with us?"

"Of course." Andrei straightened up, a broader smile than any Svetlana had seen so far on his face. "Thank you, Comrade."

"I'll come too," Svetlana exclaimed.

Krasnov shook his head, but she persisted.

"I have had nurse training. I can help!" This was a white lie, but Krasnov looked persuadable.

"We do have a sickness here," he muttered. "All right. Vadim, bring them some chow. I'll be back."

He swept out of the room, the tails of his greatcoat flying like an eagle's wings.

Surly Vadim plunked a steaming pot and two spoons on the table. The thin gruel inside was almost exactly the color of the dirty snow outside. Svetlana tasted it and made a face. It seemed like a tiny bit of rancid butter had been used to flavor gallons of water boiled with a handful of buckwheat. Wasn't this the countryside where all the food was supposed to come from? She was hungry, though, she choked down a couple of spoons. Andrei ate mechanically but polished off the rest. He did not look at Svetlana. Was he angry with her? Why? She had not behaved in any way unbecoming to a battlefield nurse. What right did he have, anyway? He was not her father or brother.

A commotion outside made them both sit up. The door flew open, and a woman burst in, discolored rags swaddling her body and making her look like an upright postal package. In her arms she held another, smaller, package.

"Comrades," the woman cried shrilly. "Pity an innocent babe. Mercy for a poor child!"

She thrust the small package at them. It reeked of

dirty diapers. From between the folds of cloth a shrunken face stared with sightless eyes at the ceiling.

Svetlana backed off. The woman dropped to her knees, striking her forehead on the floor.

"Take him," she pleaded, her piercing voice drilling into Svetlana's eardrums. "Take him, please!"

Vadim the Patrolman burst in and tried to drag the woman out, but she resisted, clinging with an unexpected strength to Svetlana's legs. The woman's hands were bloated and translucent, as if her body was filled with dishwater instead of blood. Her kerchief slipped off, exposing the pink scalp between thin tufts of hair. Throughout the scene, the baby was silent. Andrei picked him up and shook his head. The woman dissolved into hiccupping sobs and Vadim finally managed to maneuver her out.

"Demi-kulak?" Svetlana asked, breathless. She had read about this particular variety of the fists—their faces more or less human but a tightly packed egg-sack filled with the larvae of their voracious young protruding from under the breastbone.

Andrei shrugged and turned away.

"Maybe," he said in a toneless voice. "The baby was dead, though."

THE FISTS

WRAPPED UP IN their outer clothing again, they followed Krasnov and Vadim into the hush of the village. It was not evening yet, but the glassy air had a subtle admixture of darkness in it like ink dissolving in water. The sun was a pale pink smear on the white sky.

Krasnov was explaining the situation in the village and Svetlana listened with pleasure, reassured by the firm cadences of his speech. It was blasphemy to compare any man's voice with the Voice, but she thought, privately, that if anybody's could measure up, it would be Krasnov's. Perhaps it was better not to dwell too much on what he was saying. It was just too grim.

"We fulfilled our grain and milk quota early in the fall. Everything was just fine. And then . . . this disease. People dying. We requested help from Blue Meadow—that's the regional center—and they promised to send people but then . . . communication lines are down. I personally fried one damager, but who knows how many are lurking here? And the Fists are coming back, damn them, infiltrating from the Wastelands! No Patrols, not enough torches, little electricity. We have lost four men in the last three weeks. It's down to Vadim and myself."

Svetlana thought, admiringly, how brave he was to defend his village alone, supported only by his surly underling who had barely said two words since he had taken them from the train station. But now they were here, Andrei and herself, and though she would not be deterred from her purpose, surely it would help her in her petition to the Voice if she had the record of fighting the Enemy in the countryside. She remembered her assigned role of a nurse.

"What disease?" she asked, trying to sound professional. "What are the symptoms?"

Krasnov smiled at her and even in the deceptive twilight she was sure she saw kindness in his eyes.

"You'll see," he said.

They stopped in front of a big house. Its door was elaborately carved with flowers and painted red. Snow picked out the blowzy petals of the carving. Krasnov motioned to Vadim to stand aside and with one powerful kick, blew the door open.

Darkness spilled from the inside, together with the smell of dusty hay and rotten eggs. The windowless mudroom was piled up with sticks and old clothes.

"Open up," Krasnov yelled. "Patrol!"

There was no answer. Vadim stepped forward and Svetlana saw that he held a metallic rod that telescoped out into a long thin probe. With it, he pushed at the inner door that swung open with no resistance.

They walked into a large living room, choked by heavy furniture, and decorated with a profusion of embroidered wall hangings. In the dimness, tables, chairs and sofas blurred into lumped masses of shadows. Svetlana automatically searched for candles or better still an electric switch, until she realized, with revulsion, that the room had no obvious means of lighting.

Krasnov's torch cut through the gloom and she saw something whitish stir in the far corner and advance, tottering, into the center of the room. It was a girl, perhaps a couple of years older than Svetlana, slovenly and unwashed. She had only a soiled white shift on. At first, Svetlana thought the girl was overweight, but she soon realized that though her belly was as tight as a drum against her shift, her arms were knobby and emaciated. Her ankles hung in bloated folds of flesh over her bare feet.

"Stand aside," Krasnov commanded. The girl did not react, her flat eyes focusing on something above his head. Vadim, meanwhile, knelt at the hearth and pushed his metallic probe into the cracks between the floorboards.

Was the girl sick? Svetlana stepped toward her when Vadim grunted and leaned onto the probe. Something cracked.

"Here it is," he yelled.

A couple of things happened simultaneously. Shuffling footsteps came from the depth of the house, and another door creaked open. An old man stood there, leaning on the jamb, his body crossing the rectangle of the doorway at an odd angle. His chest was bare and wrapped with black shadows that twitched in the torchlight like fat leeches. His face reminded Svetlana of the dead baby—it was both intense and empty, the parchment skin tight on the cheekbones and receding from the deep wells of his eyes. He had a scruffy beard that hung almost to the waistband of his stained canvas trousers.

"Please," the man whispered and then subsided in a heap onto the floor in a strangely graceful motion. Vadim was tearing up the floorboards, uncovering a hollow brimming with darkness. Krasnov kept his torch trained on the old man, pinning him to the threshold. And the girl . . .

Svetlana squinted into the murk, sure that her eyes played a trick on her, in this dark house filled with restless shadows. The girl shuddered convulsively as if she was about to collapse just like the old man, but this was not what was happening. The girl vibrated like a plucked spring, the frequency increasing, until there was just a blur, a handful of obscure motion, writhing darkness, and then there were two girls standing in the middle of the room, their arms linked as if they were about to step out into the dancefloor. Their white shifts pulled apart and one of them sprinted across the room, toward Vadim who did not even have the time to turn around before she was upon him, her skeletal hands locked around his throat. The second one—her double, her mirror reflection—was on her knees by the hollow, plunging her arms deep into it and bringing up handfuls of glister that she crammed into her cavernous mouth. Krasnov's torch jerked, throwing a web of confusing shadows around the room, but in its stroboscopic flash Svetlana saw the old man crawl toward them, his elbows sticking into the air like the joints of a grasshopper. Then another old man, his reflection, sunk his teeth into Krasnov's leg, and the torch flew through the air in a strangely slow motion, tumbling end over end.

Svetlana still had time to think, I need to catch it, but then the torch fell with a dull crack and the room was in darkness. Only the white gleam of the snow outside, and a medley of sucking, slurping noises, and Vadim's swearing that dissolved into a thin inarticulate squeal remained.

Svetlana fell onto her knees and groped through the tangle of hostile furniture, lost in the gloom. A boot stepped onto her hand and she yelped but it was pushed off by something that smelled of a dead cat. Teeth grazed her ear. She finally grasped the cool ribbed body of a torch and pushed the round button. A spear of Light pierced the chaos.

The first thing she saw was a glistening ribbon crawling toward her. Svetlana's brain automatically went through the categories of the Enemy, trying to classify it, until she realized it was blood spilling from Vadim. He lay on his back and the old man—one of them—lapped at his torn throat. The other one was grappling with Andrei who huffed, his face alarmingly flushed, as he tried to bend back the Fist's skeletal fingers wrapped around his neck. The creature must be as strong as an ox, Svetlana thought distantly, except an ox had no fingers, did it?

The beam swept around the room and she saw Krasnov. He was down on his knees, pushing away one of the girls. She sank her teeth into his thigh and worried at it like a dog. Her shift was streaked with red. The other girl was still at the hiding place uncovered by Vadim, gulping down handfuls of what Svetlana realized was grain. She swelled visibly, ballooning into a gross parody of a woman. The oily pink skin on her arm split like the casing of a boiled hotdog.

The torch shook in Svetlana's hands that had never

held an instrument of Light before. It was surprisingly heavy, her fingers fighting to find a purchase on its slick surface. One of them. She could only help one of them? Who?

Andrei was suspicious, an enigma . . . Krasnov was responsible for this entire village, a lonely hero. Krasnov who had looked at her . . . Krasnov . . .

She turned around and sprinted through the wave of mewling shadows that rose from the floor like a tide. Toward Andrei.

She lifted the torch and trained it on the Fist that was strangling the life out of him. She had seen the Patrolmen in her house do it when her Dad . . . The memory fled, and she was fully in the moment again, watching with grim satisfaction how the assumed humanity was sloughing off the creature's face, running down in rivulets of filth, and its real visage was emerging. A clenched fist with the hole of a toothy mouth in the middle. It gave an ululating cry and let go of Andrei who promptly smashed it against the wall. It slid down in a maroon slick and lay still.

The room was filling with a morass of tiny bodies, spilling from the inner doorway. She pointed the beam down and saw hairy hides and naked tails. Rats?

No, they were walking on two legs, their clawed fingers reaching toward her, their beady eyes glittering in doll-like faces. They nibbled at her boots and tried to bite through the tough leather. Svetlana stomped and kicked, looking out for the second-stage kosmops with their slavering maws, but they were nowhere to be seen.

Krasnov was sprawled on the floor.

The girl had let go of him and joined her twin at the

grain hiding-hole. Both of them were swelling visibly as they devoured the food hidden from the requisition teams.

For a heart-stopping moment, Svetlana thought Krasnov was dead, but then he stirred as the torch-beam played over his prostrate body, clearing away the chittering hordes of rat-like manikins. He sat up. His face was daubed with blood, but the worst wound was on his thigh. Torn flesh hung in tatters, a white gleam of bone showing through the red.

"Kill them!" He pointed at the gorging twins. "Now, before they . . . "

One of them exploded.

The bloated sausage body flew apart, releasing a thin jet of foul-smelling liquid and several squirming creatures that fell into the mass of kosmops. Svetlana expected them to devour the larvae, but they did not. Instead, they were swarming over the naked bodies as if trying to keep them warm. One of the larvae started crying, then another. They sounded as deceptively baby-like as they looked.

Svetlana rushed toward them, ready to stomp them into the ground, but Andrei's hand landed on her shoulder.

"No," he said quietly. He pulled the torch out of her hand and played it over the other twin girl who shrunk under the Light and tried to crawl away, into the darkness of the house. Krasnov, holding himself up against the wall, seized a heavy chair and sent it flying into her. Her head broke up like a ripe watermelon.

Svetlana turned away, swallowing her nausea, and then went over to Krasnov whose face was the color of ash. She helped him to a chair and tearing apart her own kerchief, put a makeshift tourniquet over his savaged leg. This was clumsily done, and blood immediately soaked the thick fabric, but it was better than nothing. By the time she was finished, Andrei came back from the interior of the house, the Light from his torch blinding in her face.

"Nobody there," he said.

Svetlana looked at where the Fist larvae had been dropped but they had disappeared, together with the swarm of kosmops who must have carried them away. Or did Andrei hide them? No, that was impossible.

Krasnov hobbled toward the black hole in the floor and lifted out a handful of dusty grain.

"No matter what we did," he said, shaking his head. "We went around every house, checked everything, confiscated every loaf of bread, every egg, every chicken those monsters tried to hide. We fed the cities. Still, it's not enough. Just let them taste a little grain and you see what they do—multiply like bloody worms! The more you cut them down, the more you get."

Svetlana remembered, with a shiver of disgust, the two identical women they had shared the berth with.

"You need to lie down," she said, trying to infuse her shaking voice with medical authority.

"I guess. Well, we are done here. I'll have somebody come back for Vadim; his family will want to bury him."

Andrei offered his shoulder to Krasnov, and together he and Svetlana managed to bring him out into the crisp winter night. They half-carried, half-walked him to his own house—a hovel on the outskirts of the village. He fell heavily into bed, while Svetlana boiled water in the kitchen. Andrei checked out the empty larder.

"So, this was the disease he was talking about," she said, just to break the uncomfortable silence that grew between them. "Twinning".

Andrei shook his head.

"No," he said. "Hunger."

INTO THE WASTELANDS

TRAINS DID NOT run anymore.

They had spent a day at the Little Wells station, huddling around the small tin stove that filled the waiting-room with soporific heat. Outside, the ragged icicles were melting and dripping, fat drops of water drumming on the asphalt. The air smelled raw and tender. A thaw had come.

They spoke little. After the confrontations with the Fists, Andrei seemed to have withdrawn into himself. He spent most of the time cleaning and reassembling the black fire-stick that he called the Nagant.

Svetlana was repulsed by its oily sheen that resembled an Enemy's skin, its aura of sly darkness. She had seen how deadly it could be, but Andrei told her that it only held two more shots to fire. What use was such a weapon compared with the generosity of Light? But Svetlana did not tell him that. The distance between them seemed to be growing with every empty minute they spent waiting for the train that did not come.

Krasnov, laid up in his shabby house, his leg swollen and the brow running with fever-sweat, was another unspoken topic. Svetlana had gone several times to visit him but the round-faced young woman with a long brown braid who had taken residence by his bedside made it clear she was not welcome. The woman's name was Nina; she was Krasnov's fiancée, and she could do the same kind of nursing as Svetlana—changing bandages and putting a cold rag on his forehead to bring down fever—tolerably well.

The fat conductor who had removed them from the train haunted the station like an unhappy ghost, poking his head into the waiting-room as if to check that they had not absconded with the stove or the chipped tea-mug that hung on a chain from the wall. When the conductor checked on them for the fifth time, Andrei invited him in. They drank tea, passing the mug around. They were the only ones there. The other passengers who had been taken off the train had been sent back to Loadstone Rock.

"How?" Svetlana asked.

The conductor shrugged and pointed to the tracks that snaked through the snow toward the invisible horizon.

"Walking," he said.

They probably did not get very far.

They had the conductor to thank for the sledge. Once it became clear that no train would come any time soon, they had to decide what to do. Andrei was in favor of staying in Little Wells for a while, perhaps lending a hand to the authorities—the much-depleted Village Council—until Krasnov was back in service. Svetlana was adamantly opposed. Every minute spent here was a minute the Enemy was using to tighten its grip on her city and her parents.

But how to get out? Even though the bitter cold had

abated, roads leading to the City of Light were all but impassable. Except by a troika.

Svetlana, having lived in a city her entire life, knew of a troika—three horses harnessed abreast and pulling a sledge—only from books. But for the conductor it was a mundane means of transportation, a fallback for when the trains, which he still regarded with awe, would finally stop running. Clearly such a miracle could not continue forever, and the current interruption of service was, for him, a restoration of the detested but familiar status quo. He had a large beat-up sledge in his barn, its blades greased and stained red. He was willing to sell it to Andrei—he conspicuously refused to negotiate with Svetlana, treating her as if she were Andrei's shadow. The idea of a sale was repugnant—only foreigners and other Enemy allies used money on a regular basis—but there was some paper currency in the bag she had packed in her apartment. As for horses, nobody could spare three, of course, but there was a swaybacked little mare whose future lay in the cooking pot, or with Andrei and Svetlana.

So, they found themselves in the creaking sledge out on the snow-covered plane, their legs hidden under the moth-eaten rug and their mare wheezing in her efforts, occasionally stopping to cast a reproachful glance at her passengers and then trotting on. Harnessing, feeding, and steering were all done by Andrei who knew exactly what to do with this strange animal. Svetlana, on the other hand, felt awkward and superfluous. Pouting at his competence, she stared morosely at the featureless cover of white that spread around them, blending with the sky the color of a dove's breast. The weather had changed again. High clouds mantled the sky, and the snow was crisp and glittering with ice crystals.

They did not have far to go. The closest village, Big Wells, was only five kilometers away. As its name indicated, it was a bigger place than Little Wells, and hopefully they still had lines of communication intact.

Svetlana thought about this a lot. She would have to deliver her information through the black tube of a far-speaker. Would it carry the same impact as when delivered in person? Would anybody listen to her? Her initial plan involved walking boldly into the House of the People and demanding a personal audience with the Voice. She had imagined herself striding fearlessly through the marble halls in the halo of Light, and then standing in the presence of . . . well, the Voice. At this point her fantasy abruptly shut down, confronted with the blankness of her ignorance. Now she knew she would have to deal with actual people, Patrolmen or officials, and she worried that they would treat her as a hysterical little girl.

But Krasnov had believed her—or perhaps, had believed Andrei. Her dependence on him rankled her but the bond between them was as palpable and incontrovertible as the bond she had had with her parents. For the first time, she realized that even if her Dad had truly been corrupted by the Enemy, she would hate and despise him—but she would still be his daughter.

As for Andrei, he seemed to have made his peace with reality. She no longer saw him stare with that intent, glassy eyes at ordinary objects, such as torches or loudspeakers, as if trying to pierce their disguise.

He had agreed with her that the first priority was to inform the Voice of the eyeless infestation and then to abide by his decision. But there was a strange passivity in his agreement, which she did not like. Surely, information was just the first step. She had no doubt that the Voice would send POP forces to Loadstone Rock to deliver her parents, and she was resolved to go with them. But she was not sure what he would do.

These thoughts kept her awake, despite the rhythmic swaying of the sledge and the vast silence that enveloped them. Andrei was awake as well, peering at the cloud-smudged horizon where the night was rising in a slow tide.

"The City of Light has electric streetlights on every street and electric bulbs in every apartment," Svetlana said, trying to dispel the vague sense of something large and faceless looming over them.

Andrei nodded distractedly.

"And food," Svetlana added. "Lots of food. Fresh bread, cottage cheese, sausage, yellow butter."

She had never been as hungry in her entire life as she was now. Loadstone Rock, a factory town, was well-provisioned. The starvation of Little Wells shook her but not enough to wonder about the source of their own plentiful rations.

"Yeah, sure." Andrei pulled on the reins as the mare stopped and then started again at a faster clip. "Listen, Sveta . . . this Voice . . . "

"Yes?"

"Is he . . . a man?"

Svetlana was scandalized by the question.

"He is our Leader."

"Yes, I understand. But what is he?"

"He protects and defends Motherland. He speaks words of fire and they become sparks of Light. He—"

Andrei pressed his finger to his lips, and pulled on the reins, bringing the horse to a stop. Suspended in the fading light, a tiny mote on the sparkling plain, they listened.

And heard. A low mournful howling, rolling over the snow.

"Wolves," Andrei exclaimed and urged the mare forward.

Svetlana peered into the thickening murk. Wolves?

The noise was strangely regular, almost articulate. Despite its seemingly nearness, she could not see any canine shapes against the white.

Something moved at the edge of her vision—a confused mass of shadows. It did not look like a wolf pack. They were heading straight toward it, though. It rose and fell with a monotonous beat like an ocean wave stranded in the middle of dry land. The howling intensified and now it was clear it was not an animal sound. There was something mechanical in it.

"What the f—What the hell is it?" Andrei exclaimed.

Svetlana squinted, her eyes tearing up as the cold nipped at her cheeks and nose. In the deceptive snow-glow, the shadowy mass blurred into the bruised sky. Tendrils of fog danced in front of them, appearing out of nowhere. Svetlana touched the reassuring coldness of the torch Krasnov had given them. Andrei pulled out his Nagant.

A whiff of warm air caressed her cheek, an unnatural spring suddenly coming in the middle of a cold spell. The snow around them was visibly melting.

The sledge suddenly skewed, vibrated. The horse strained in her harness, pulling against the quagmire. They were stranded on a patch of bare ground, gluey with meltwater. Steam rose from the ground. The drifts were deflating, dissolving into rivulets. Heat wafted into her face like a dragon's breath.

The horse began to panic, her eyes rolling in her head, her steaming breath blending with the gusts of steam blowing at them. The howling still went on, rising and falling with the regularity of a metronome, the steam spurting up in unison with the sound.

Andrei jumped out of the sledge and tried to calm the spooked mare, which flailed around, hooves striking at random, the muzzle covered with foam.

A bluish glow dawned ahead like a misplaced moonrise. The horse, maddened by the howling, struck out at Andrei who managed to leap back, trying to grab the harness. But it snapped and the horse tore through the snow, disappearing in the night.

Svetlana joined Andrei. They picked up their bags and trudged through the slush. The temperature was steadily rising until Svetlana pulled down her woolen scarf, wiping off the sweat that beaded her face.

They walked toward an indistinct cloud squatting on the plain, its core pulsating with a pale light and radiating heat. The howling, coming from inside it, was unquestioningly mechanical, like a demented factory bell. From time to time, plumes of steam shot from the cloud high into the sky where they dissipated into a murky fog. Condensation sprinkled their faces like a rain out of season.

They did not talk; even if the howling were not so loud, there was nothing to say. Without their horse, they were stranded in the middle of the snow plain. Ahead was the only way to go.

Svetlana's boots were filled with sloshing water by the time they came closer to the cloud.

Granny Olga would have had a fit; she always believed that getting your feet wet was the surest way to get a bad cold and die. She herself died on a bright and sunny day, while bringing her granddaughter to the crèche. A wave of her hand as little Sveta ran toward her one-candle group leader, and then Granny collapsed on the pavement, felled by a sudden stroke.

Svetlana did not know why this memory came so vividly to her as they finally stood in front of the howling wall of steam. Flashes of blue radiance periodically lit up the white billows. The snow was gone; the ground was sodden and bare.

Andrei took her hand and together they stepped into the cloud.

THE PIT

THE COILING STEAM closed around them like a fog bank—a suffocating blankness that stank of hot iron and rust. They groped through, holding hands.

Svetlana's face burned with the heat.

Then the blankness ended abruptly. They stepped out and found themselves on the lip of a large excavation surrounded by a belt of raw earth. There were several skeletal watchtowers around the excavation, each topped with a revolving searchlight. Their illumination looked like a mockery of the buttery warmth of electricity: harsh and lifeless. The howling seemed to come from these towers or rather from the searchlights, as if this dead glare screamed its own unnaturalness into the night.

Svetlana's fingers closed convulsively around Krasnov's electric torch, but she did not turn it on. The sense that they were being watched by mocking and hostile eyes was overwhelming.

She lingered, frightened of approaching the excavation, seeing what it contained. Andrei stepped forward and looked down. Even through a renewed burst of howling she could hear his gasp.

There was nothing to do but look. It took maybe a

couple of seconds to walk to the edge, but each second expanded into hours' worth of memory. Mama and Dad; Granny Olga; her schoolroom with a scratched blackboard and chalk dust on the floor; the ceremony of three candles; the lost notebook; Tattie . . .

Yes, Tattie as she had seen her last. Eyeless. With a bleeding hole in her chest.

She looked down.

The pit was filled with corpses.

It was a large concave hole in the ground, its sides scooped out of the frozen earth. Up to two-thirds of its depth, filled with bodies like pale grubs, thrown carelessly over each other, heaped up in a generosity of slaughter. All naked. It reminded her of the communal bathhouse she had gone to with her mother and the profusion of jiggling female flesh that had embarrassed her so much she had kept her eyes closed as she walked and collided with an indignant older woman. There was the steam too, wreathing over the bodies, and for a foolish second, she almost made herself believe it was some weird sauna . . . but the bodies here were of both sexes and all ages. And they were dead.

Andrei was swearing, using words she did not know existed, but his voice was coming from afar. It was as if this was the pivot, the culminating moment of her journey when she came face to face with reality. Everything else that had happened, yes, even her father's arrest, had been wrapped up in a layer of words that cushioned its impact. Not here. This was what it was and nothing else.

"Sveta! These are not people, right? These are some weird . . . whatever you call them . . . shapeshifters? Kosmops? Whatever?"

She shook her head. They were not the Enemy. They were people.

In the flashes of searchlights, she saw them with perfect clarity: their skinny legs, pathetic paunches, and sagging breasts. They lay exposed and defenseless, every pretense of civilized living having been stripped away from him. They had no need of modesty anymore.

There were quite a lot of children, tucked in among the adult bodies. One of them was clutching a doll. She stared at it because there was no other man-made object in the pit, but then realized it was not a doll but a baby.

The bodies were capriciously daubed with smears and stains. Paint? Svetlana leaned closer, as if understanding all of this could somehow make it disappear.

Not paint. Each of the bodies had a neat round hole as if they had been drilled by a thorough mechanic. Most of the holes were in the forehead but some, especially children, had them in the chest or abdomen. Sluggish frozen blood dripped from the holes, black in the colorless illumination.

"They were shot," Andrei said. "You told me you had no guns in your world."

The suspicion in his voice cut her to the core and she whipped around, ready to give him an appropriate tongue-lashing . . . and then she was in his arms, torn with dry sobbing.

"I'm sorry, little sister," he whispered. "Sorry you had to see this."

The howling suddenly stopped, and the silence was as loud as a scream.

Andrei pointed to the nearest watchtower.

There was somebody up there, by the searchlight. The glare had diminished, fading to a dim aureole, against which the black silhouette was clearly visible. The man—for it looked like a man in a long coat—did not move. They could not see his face, but they knew he was looking at them.

Svetlana's gaze swept the rest of the towers: six all in all. On top of each, a man stood, looking down at them. She felt like a butterfly pinned to a collector's wall.

Andrei pulled out his Nagant. She heard the click of the safety.

The figures on top of the towers did not move but there was a noise behind them, many feet trampling in the snow. From beyond the curtain of steam—she still was not sure where it was coming from—came a column of shuffling, bent figures.

They were people, dressed in ragged burlap shirts and pants, their bare feet ice-blue. They passed so close to Svetlana and Andrei that she could have touched a chicken-thin arm or a hunched shoulder. The people paid them no attention. A couple of them jumped into the pit, landing on the heap of corpses, and started lifting them up like so much firewood, and throwing them over the edge. The rest of the ragged people composed a chain-gang, passing bodies along until the last of them loaded them onto a sort of wagon and pulled them toward a low barrack-like building that squatted beyond the watchtower. Svetlana had not seen it before because there was not a shred of illumination coming out of its windows. It was just a featureless shape, black on black.

Svetlana's cry sat in her throat like a stone. She had forced it back when she saw the ragged people's faces, their eyes supplanted by spiky, squirming, sooty stars.

TRAITORS

The cell was filthy.

There was dry vomit on the floor where its previous inhabitant had emptied his or her guts. The bucket in the corner filled the tiny space with stench. At least, it was too cold for flies. Svetlana could imagine the cell buzzing with insects in summer.

She sat on the edge of the bunk that held a scrunched-up dirty blanket which she refused to touch, overwhelmed by the disgust toward its no-doubt-dead-now previous user. It was as if the blanket crawled with the detritus of the body that refused to recognize its demise.

She was cold, though, so cold that after a while the idea of snuggling into this corpse-blanket began to appear rational. Why not? Would she be better off frozen to death? Didn't she owe it to her city, her family, and the Voice to survive and learn as much as possible? A three-candles girl, almost an adult, there were more important things in life than getting a little dirt over her clothes, which were not the cleanest to begin with.

Still, the disgust was so strong that she kept making bargains with herself before giving in and wrapping herself up in the corpse-blanket.

I will wait ten minutes, five minutes, three ...

Besides helping to pass the time, the bargaining also left a little less room in her mind for thinking about Andrei.

They had been separated immediately when the guards came down from the watchtowers. Andrei had readied his gun but then stuffed it back into the holster. There were two bullets left and six guards.

Had they taken his gun away? They would know what it was because they had guns of their own. They looked a little different from Andrei's but worked on the same principle. Svetlana had seen it when one of them shot an eyeless worker who had slipped and let the corpse he was handling fall into the snow. There was a sharp crack and the man keeled over, a patch of blood blossoming over his midriff. Just like Tattie.

The guards were human. This was the one fact she could not wrap her head around. Even the dead in the pit had not been as horrifying as what she had seen when the six men surrounded them, their guns drawn. Everybody knew the Enemy killed people. What she had witnessed in Little Wells had been excruciating but not surprising.

But the sneering men that pulled her away from Andrei had bland ordinary faces. One had zits. Another, a little goatee. Still another was older and mildly overweight. Their eyes were human eyes, albeit cruel and mocking. Svetlana tried to convince herself there was a sooty star hiding at the bottom of their pupils, but she knew there were none.

One of the men twisted her arm so far back that she heard the bone crack. Andrei lunged toward her but was held back by the rest.

They did not speak. The silence was so unnerving that while they were marching her to the long, low building, she tried to talk to them, even calling them "comrades". She instantly hated herself for that. Whatever they were, they were not comrades.

But what were they? A new kind of Enemy? Impossible! One of the rules of unmasking the Enemy was that there was always a physical mark, a difference, however subtle. Even oborotni who could pass at a casual glance invariably revealed their true nature when exposed to Light.

But there were human traitors. Collaborators. This was also known. One of the main functions of POP was rooting out those despicable humans who sold their birthright of Light for food or power or even money.

Svetlana remembered her father and recoiled from this thought with an almost physical revulsion.

Her Dad, like all the people of Loadstone Rock, like the corpse-bearers, had been infected. Possessed. He was blameless. Not a traitor but a victim. This had happened before. In one of her classes, they had learned about the history of Motherland: the coming of the Voice, the struggle against the forces of Darkness, the waves of attacks by the Enemy. At the time, the Enemy had worn different disguises from the ones she was familiar with. She was pretty sure an infestation or possession had been discussed. Once again, she bitterly regretted not paying enough attention, losing her notebook. If she could just go back to the time when the world, cleanly divided between Light and Darkness, had made perfect sense, she would be twice as industrious, three times as dedicated, and ten times as careful! She would give everything to be the girl she had been before.

Before she met Andrei.

Every train of thought she followed seemed to lead her back into a thicket of doubt and pain. Shivering, she picked up the blanket and draped it over her shoulders. It smelled of dandruff.

When the guards had taken them into the windowless building, she had been shocked to see it was brightly lit inside. The second shock was the nature of this illumination. It was not electric Light. Soulless and flat, it leached colors and turned faces into plaster masks. It had no obvious source, dribbling from wall edges. It cast no shadows and made no connections, reducing everything it touched to a random accumulation of ugly objects. But perhaps even natural daylight would not be able to smooth the ugliness of what was inside the building.

She and Andrei had been led on a shaky walkway above an enormous room like an industrial hangar. Below were rectangular boxes filled with some steaming reddish goo. On top of the goo grew a web of black filaments, like a mushroom farm. Indeed, there were fruiting bodies, lifting off the matrix as they grew: sooty, spiky stars. Eyeless people were moving between the rows of boxes, adding more reddish goo. They were taking it from the large pool in the corner where a sturdy pipe occasionally cleared its mechanical throat and ejected blobs of the stuff. The pipe was connected to a large mechanical contraption outside, where Svetlana had seen eyeless slaves load dead bodies onto its conveyor belt.

The door to her cell suddenly flew open and a man shoved a tin plate and a mug inside. Svetlana took a step toward the man, trying to catch his eye, smiling.

The ingrained habit of the lifetime spent in the world cleanly divided between humanity and the Enemy was too hard to break.

He snarled and pushed her back with such force that she fell against the edge of the bunk, bruising her spine. He was gone by the time Svetlana picked up the plate to discover it filled with porridge. She resolved to reject the food, but she was starving and the hot smell that filled her nostrils was like paradise in this reeking prison. She polished off the porridge. It was richer and better tasting than the thin gruel of Little Wells.

She kept replaying the man's snarl in her mind. Was it an indication that he was not human, after all? Didn't he sound more like an animal . . . ?

Actually, it sounded like a word. But a word in a language she did not know.

***

Svetlana dozed off, despite the unchanging glare—she would not call it light—that kept her in a state of restless agitation. The sound of footsteps in the corridor outside her cell woke her up.

The door flew open, and a man stepped in.

"Sveta!" he said.

It was her father.

TWO SHOTS

SHE WAS SNIFFLING into his shoulder, while his familiar smell—sawdust and wool—dispelled the stench of the prison cell, and his familiar hands patted her back awkwardly, just as they had done in the long-ago childhood when her greatest sorrows had been a lost sand-bucket or a slingshot from the neighborhood's bad boy. These hands had made everything all right then.

"Daddy," she sobbed.

"Come on, Sveta, you are a big girl now. Everything will be fine. Don't cry."

His voice sounded pinched somehow and she instantly felt ashamed. Surely, his tribulations had been worse than hers.

"Mama . . . " she whispered.

"Your mother is here too. You are going to see her soon."

She straightened up, tried to wipe her eyes, smearing tears and snot all over her face. It sounded like a dream. Could it be a dream? No, it was all too rough, too real. She was cold, and hungry, and in need of a bath—and her father was here!

"Mama is here?"

"Yes. We are going to her now."

He took her hand and led her out of the cell, the door hanging open, the fearsome locks defanged by his mere touch.

Outside, in the corridor lined with more doors, she stopped, disoriented. When the men had brought them into this annex of their infernal factory, they had pushed Andrei into an adjacent cell, but she could not locate Andrei's cell now.

"Daddy," she tugged on his hand like a little girl. "Wait! Andrei is here."

He half-turned toward her, his glasses glowing with the reflection of the luminescent ceiling.

"The man who was with you?"

There was something awkward about the way he said it, as if he was trying to shape a different sentence and bit back the superfluous parts.

"Yes, Andrei. The soldier. Remember the soldier I brought home when—"

And then it all came flooding back.

"Dad!" She stopped. "Dad!"

"Come on, Sveta. They are waiting."

"Who? Dad, how did you come here? What are you doing?"

Her father just walked faster, and she ran after him, breathless.

"What are you doing here? Who are these people? Where is Mama?"

At the end of the corridor was another door. Her father pushed it open.

It was another windowless cell but larger and cleaner, containing a scrubbed table and a couple of chairs. A woman wrapped up in a large down shawl sat at the table, vacantly staring at her hands. She stirred when Svetlana and her father entered and lifted her head. All her movements were slow and sluggish as if she were waking up from deep slumber.

"Mama!" Svetlana rushed to her.

The woman's arms, swathed in the folds of her shawl, lifted awkwardly and went around Svetlana's back. Then they dropped.

Svetlana backed off, staring at the woman.

"Mama . . . ?" she said softly.

The edge of the shawl was pulled down low over the woman's brow, shadowing her eyes.

She looked back at her father who stood by the door, leaning woodenly against the wall. Her parents had not acknowledged each other in any way.

Svetlana went over to her father and snatched the glasses off his nose. He tried to forestall her, but all his movements were slow and off-phase.

She dropped the glasses on the floor and the lenses shattered.

"So," Svetlana whispered, "they were right. The Patrol. When they came . . . "

Her legs seemed to be made of cotton wool as she sat down heavily. Her mother—or the creature that masqueraded as her mother—made a strange abortive gesture, as if trying to reach out to her and missing the target.

"They only want what's best for us," the eyeless puppet with the face of her father said.

"Who are they?" she asked. It did not matter, nothing mattered anymore, but she had to know. Why? She was not sure. At least it was something to break the crushing silence.

"They come to liberate us," the mother-puppet said. Even her voice—squeaky and disused—did not sound like her anymore.

"Come from where?"

"Another country. A better country."

"Wulfstan," Svetlana said. She did not know how she knew, but it fit.

They were silent.

"What do you want from me?"

"You are our daughter," the father-puppet said. "You have to be with us. As a family."

"A family," the mother-puppet echoed. Her hand was crawling on the tabletop as if independent of her—a small furtive animal. She looked down at it and slapped it with her other hand. Her transformation had not gone as far as that of Svetlana's father: he had empty holes where his eyes had been but hers harbored black furry spiders quivering inside her irises.

I'm an orphan now, Svetlana thought dully. It's not too bad to be an orphan. The Voice is our father. I don't need anybody else. Not mother, father, or . . .

I had a sister named Sveta.

My sister was a pest.

I bet you are a good girl . . .

Andrei! The cry in her mind was so loud that she was sure the eyeless puppets would hear it, but they did not stir. Brother! Help!

A door banged in the corridor and a medley of shouts erupted outside. Something heavy crashed into the wall. A sharp crack echoed through the building. The puppets did not react.

Andrei crashed into the room. There was blood on

his cheek and his clothes were in tatters. He slammed the door, turned the lock. A hail of blows fell onto the sturdy metal plate, but it held.

The puppets moved.

The mother-puppet lunged across the table and caught Andrei's arm. He shook her away. The father-puppet rushed at him from behind and fastened to his back like a leech, trying to sink his teeth into his neck. Andrei tried to reach back and tear him away, but the creature caught his arm and twisted it. The mother-puppet dropped to her belly and crawled under the table, her teeth snapping as she sought the vulnerable flesh above his shredded boots.

"Nagant!" Svetlana yelled.

With his one free hand, Andrei tossed the gun across the room, and she caught it.

She had seen Andrei do it. It was easy.

Aim, pull the trigger, fire.

Two shots rang out. The two last bullets were spent.

ON THE MARCH

THEY HAD BEEN marching for two days now. They had been marching for two days now through unstable weather. Brief periods of thaw interspersed with blasts of icy air from the north froze the slush into a slippery mudflat. At least they were lucky it did not snow, even though a snowstorm could bring warmer air in its wake. But they needed visibility.

On the way they found several burnt villages. They were so thoroughly ransacked that not even a trace of the Enemy-hidden food remained. Nor was there an Enemy to be seen. They had all joined the Wulfstan troops.

The gaunt-faced soldiers had instantly accepted Andrei as one of their own. They shared hand-rolled makhorka cigarettes, and easy banter, and a swallow of homemade throat-burning spirits from a milk bottle in the evening. They did not quite know what to make of Svetlana and treated her with an almost ridiculous courtesy. It suited her just fine because it kept them at a distance. She did not feel like talking to anybody.

They were walking toward the City of Light where the Voice had called upon all the defenders of Motherland to take their stand. Trains were not running, for the most part, because the Enemy had sabotaged the lines, blowing up the tracks and derailing both passenger and supply cars. Fortunately, they were not too far from the capital, and this part was free from the occupying troops.

Sometimes, when the unstable clouds parted, and a patch of the washed-out sky was cleared, Svetlana saw mechanical blackbirds flap their giant wings, their shadows sliding over the platoon like a momentary night. They were friendly; Wulfstan's flying machines were in the shape of a crooked-nosed eagle. Once, they witnessed an aerial fight between a blackbird and an eagle, filling the sky with a raucous mechanical cawing. Then the clouds scudded back. Later on, they found bent and scorched pieces of metal and a bloodied pilot's harness. It was not clear who it had belonged to.

A blackbird had saved Svetlana's and Andrei's lives. It had glided low over the Wulfstan death-factory, strafing the running soldiers with rays of pure Light, and then flew away, but not before depositing a polished metal egg that hatched with a noise like the popping of a cork, flooding the site with electrical discharges that fried a fair number of soldiers and eyeless slaves. The discharges had also disabled most of the locks in the prison wing. Andrei and Svetlana sneaked away in the ensuing confusion and simply ran through the wet snow just to get as far from the death-factory as possible. They ran into this depleted platoon of straggling Patrolmen, all of them recent recruits. They were caught in the crossbeams of Light that failed to do any damage beyond filling their eyes with blue afterimages, so they hardly saw the face of the POP officer who interrogated them. He turned out to be Krasnov's cousin, looking even younger and more exhausted than his kinsman. He told them there had been a raid on Little Wells soon after they had left and Krasnov was killed.

Now they and the soldiers were walking toward the City of Light, surviving on depleted rations of dark bread and hard cheese, and talking about the weather, cigarettes, and homecoming; anything except what was really on everybody's mind.

The weapons of Light, so potent against the Enemy, were useless against Wulfstan soldiers and their eyeless slaves. Both were human—or had been human—and sacred electricity had no more effect on them than on ordinary people. Indeed, some of them could apparently pervert Light and turn it into a deadly weapon. Hearing this, Svetlana remembered the blistering rays aimed upon her by the infested soldiers in Loadstone Rock.

This is not to say that electricity was useless as ammunition. The metallic egg laid by the blackbird was proof to the contrary. The country had been urgently mobilizing its resources, calling up all Patrolmen and -women, instituting 24-hour factory shifts, shooting deserters and traitors, and rooting out the proliferating hordes of the homegrown Enemy. But despite all the efforts, the Wulfstan armies swept through the heart of Motherland, laying waste to cities and villages alike. Loadstone Rock was lost. When told this, Svetlana felt nothing except a momentary dull pain like the memory of a wound.

The worst thing was that no matter how thorough the extermination of the Enemy appeared to have been, new specimens kept appearing, as if conjured up by the fear sweeping through the land. Fists ate up the stored grain; oborotni and krovososy picked up orphans and stray kids on the streets; damagers sabotaged railway tracks and communication lines; Kosmops bred like rats in bombed-out ruins. The fiery words of the Voice that were supposed to inspire the people to fight and to rout the cowardly Enemy were not available. Lines of communication were mostly down; loudspeakers were silent, mirrors were tarnished or broken, and the Voice did not send his words of fire across the land anymore. Svetlana realized, with another pang of dull pain, that she had not heard the Voice since the evening of Andrei's appearance.

They hardly talked on the march. Andrei retreated into the same deep silence that he had sought refuge in when they were in Little Wells. He did not appear to be gloomy or depressed, just thoughtful, as if he were pondering some intractable math problem. Svetlana found that she could sleep if she was sufficiently tired. Since the marching alone did not do the trick, she took charge of the battalion's depleted medical kit and dispensed aspirin, vitamins, and the unguent for blistered feet every time they pitched camp. This helped. She would gladly have taken on the cooking duty had there been anything to cook and if it meant she didn't have to remember the tableau of her parents falling onto the dirty cell floor.

They did briefly discuss what they had seen at the death factory with Krasnov's cousin whose name was Alex. The infestation of eylessness had clearly been the first stage of the planned invasion, carried out by the homegrown Enemy and human traitors and collaborators. Since information-gathering was in disarray, Alex did not know how many places were affected but it did appear that Loadstone Rock had been the epicenter.

The infestation seemed to be carried through ration cards and other paperwork, including even the rare paper money. Anything with a red star logo on it could become a vehicle. A tiny spiky star would substitute itself for the familiar and reassuring symbol, slither onto the body of whoever handled the infested object and then . . .

And then an upright, ordinary, honest citizen and worker would be infected with Darkness and become an Enemy, a traitor to Motherland. A willing slave to the perfidious Wulfstan invaders who had broken the peace treaty and mounted this devastating and cowardly attack.

Andrei glanced at her worriedly when they were discussing this subject, as if mere words could be any more disturbing than the blind faces of her family she saw every time she closed her eyes.

But the strange thing, Alex said, is that the stars were not just counterfeit logos. They seemed to be actually alive. His voice rose as he said it, in wonder and curiosity, and glancing at his eager face with the blond down on the rounded chin, Svetlana could tell that in ordinary times, he would be leading a two-candles learning group, pouring chemicals into retorts to devise a better method of Enemy's larvae extermination, or tinkering with batteries to improve the yield of torches. In ordinary times, he would be heading for the City of Light to join the Academy of

Sciences as a cadet instead of trampling through the slush and waiting to be killed. Even though he was a couple of years older than her, Svetlana felt an almost maternal tenderness toward him. Like all of her emotions nowadays, it seemed to be muted, filtered through a thick layer of depression.

But yes, Andrei responded, the stars were undoubtedly alive—parasites of some kind, like tapeworms or ticks, penetrating their hosts' brains through their eyes and turning good, dedicated citizens into . . . His voice petered out and he glanced at Svetlana again, but she completed the sentence: into the Enemy.

So, the Wulfstan death-factory must be the nursery for them, Andrei continued, something like a chicken incubator. They were grown . . . he faltered, and Svetlana completed again: in pulverized corpses.

This was valuable info, though they did not know whether it had already become common knowledge. They would find out in the City of Light. So, they pressed on through the desolate, white-shrouded countryside.

That evening, Andrei sought her out as she was counting out the remaining vitamin pills. There were five left. Some men were beginning to show signs of scurvy.

He tugged her scruffy braid and she smiled at him, but the interaction felt forced. She felt, almost physically, that they were drifting even further apart. She wanted him to go away but he did not, lowering himself onto the canvas sheet she had spread by the side of a tiny fire.

"The fritzes . . . " he said, "I mean . . . Wolfbane people . . . "

"Wulfstan," she corrected.

"Whatever. They have guns."

Svetlana looked away.

"Your . . . our people don't."

She knew what he was asking. He was right. Mutely, she pulled the Nagant out of her front pocket and gave it to him. The oily piece of metal had been lying, heavy and inescapable, against her heart since their escape.

Andrei took it with some hesitation, but she could see how well it fit into his hand.

"There are no bullets," he said.

"In the City, they will know how to make them," she said.

The next morning, they saw the train.

THE CITY

SHE HAD SEEN pictures in textbooks, of course, and sung patriotic songs about the glory of Light shining at the heart of Motherland and illuminating forests and rivers, cities and towns. The reality was different, yet not so different as to make it unrecognizable.

Peering through the dirty train window, she first saw a spiral shape etched on the clouds. It appeared small, as delicate as a seashell, dwarfed by the snowstorm massing above it. Only when Svetlana saw the twinkling lights far below did she realize the Tower of the Voice rose fifty stories high. Its twin-helix openwork body was painted in red and stood out boldly against the murky background. It leaned to the side, as if in defiance of the ordinary laws of physics and architecture, proclaiming its own invincible uniqueness. Inside the mammoth curving framework, Svetlana could discern large bodies suspended in the air and picked out by lines of bright electric lights. She knew these structures rotated once in twenty-four hours and contained meeting halls and guest houses. On top was a giant ball of Light, so bright that they said night never dared to enter the City.

Svetlana stared at the Tower, spellbound, as the

overcrowded train chugged through the fields of black earth and mushy snow. The grandeur of the view made her feel suddenly alive. By her side, Andrei stared intently through the window, his brow furrowed.

"Doesn't look like . . . " he murmured to himself. Whatever the City did not look like was swallowed in the piercing whistle of the locomotive as it pushed through the cat's cradle of tracks that converged on the City's Main Station.

When they finally disembarked at the Main Station, the chaos she had witnessed in Loadstone Rock and Little Wells was here as well, only on a larger scale. The enormous hall of the station with its stained-glass windows representing the coming of the Voice was filled with gray people wrapped up in rags and hauling suitcases and squalling children. Some were asleep in the middle of the filthy floor, their mouths agape. The station stank. A couple of harried Patrolwomen tried to direct the unruly flows of refugees without much success.

Alex and the rest of the battalion were supposed to report to the POP HQ that was situated across the road from the Main Station. Andrei and Svetlana said awkward goodbyes and slipped out of the station, relieved to be in the fresh air. The sky was turning deep winter blue and the lights along the street glowed like underwater pearls.

There were guesthouses for out-of-town visitors, but they were hopelessly crowded.

Svetlana and Andrei walked in silence down the broad avenue lined with black trees whose branches were festooned by the white lace of frost. Otherwise, the snow had been cleared away from the center of the sidewalk. The roads were clear, too, and infrequent streetcars passed by with a soft purr.

They did not talk about tomorrow. Here, surrounded by the wide avenues and tall buildings of the capital, their plans felt childish and unreal. An audience with the Voice? The Voice spoke to everybody and nobody. He was the incarnation of Light; the father of Motherland; the axis of the world. Even to think that a little girl from a provincial town could stand in his presence was presumptuous. The idea that she would boldly demand an audience was madness. Yet, Svetlana knew that this was what she was going to do because there was nothing else left for her. Giving up this goal would mean confronting the memory pit where her parents' bodies lay unburied.

The street lay before them in the festive glow of small lights draped around tall poles. Above the roofs, the Tower of the Voice glowed crimson. Svetlana noticed that the red star on top of the sphere of Light had been removed. Did it mean that even the Tower was not free of the threat of black stars?

Away from the station, the streets were surprisingly empty. She looked at the solid multistoried houses lining the avenue. Some windows glowed with the reassuring yellow of electricity but not many. What about the rest? Were the tenants gone to fight? Or . . . she remembered the Enemy-infested sealed floors of Loadstone Rock.

Andrei stopped.

"This is all very posh," he said. "Not for us, I think."

She had to agree. It did not look like there would be dorms, or guesthouses, or canteens here. The houses frowned down at them with their haughty brick faces.

They turned around and went back to the Main Station, passing a couple of bodies lying in the dirty snow scraped off to the side—unconscious, drunk, or dead.

There was an open canteen near the station, overflowing with the fug of densely packed bodies that misted the bare bulb hanging from the ceiling. Despite the late hour and the fact that some people were openly drinking, the canteen was eerily silent.

Andrei pushed through the throng with an assurance of long practice and found a place for the two of them at the edge of a long communal table.

Svetlana went over to the large soup-kettle boiling on the stove and brought two plates back. They had just started tucking in, slurping the thin but blissfully hot cabbage concoction, when a hand landed on Andrei's shoulder.

"Found you," a voice said.

It was Alex.

THE AUDIENCE

SHE BARELY NOTICED the open metalwork, as sturdy as any factory joists and as delicate as rime. She paid little attention to the marvel of the huge but silent mechanisms that gently rotated the structures within the Tower, each hanging sphere big as an average apartment block. Of the POP operatives who accompanied them through the mirror-lined corridors and into a glittering elevator, like a hollowed-out diamond, she retained only the general impression of young stern faces and long leather overcoats. All Svetlana remembered afterwards was the abundance of Light. It spilled from every giant window and skylight, gleamed on the polished marble floors and ceilings, reflected from mirrors and gilded cornices, twinkled in the garlands of tiny bulbs draped over arched doorways and blazed from the giant electric chandeliers. Light was everywhere, filling Svetlana with its promise of the bright future and washing away the grief and despair that had clogged her mind like layers of grime. She seemed to float through it, as weightless as a mote in a sunbeam. For the first time in ages, she remembered again the meaning of her name: Light.

Andrei walked tall and proud by her side, his shoulders square. He had his soldier face on—the same face that had prompted her to stand between him and the marauding Fist.

They were back to what they were meant to be doing.

"He wants to see you," Alex had said in the canteen.

"He?"

"The Voice."

They were the only survivors of Loadstone Rock. They were the only ones who had been to a Wulfstan death factory and escaped. They had valuable information.

And so here they were.

The escort stopped by the enormous double door whose bronze surface was decorated with bas-relief scenes of Motherland's struggles and victories. The door swung open noiselessly, and Svetlana and Andrei walked through. The POP escort did not follow.

At first, she thought they were out in the open air, as far up as any blackbird could fly, on the top of the leaning Tower. Then she realized that the room was, in fact, enclosed and its walls and ceiling were mirrors. Unbroken slabs of mirror-glass surrounded them on all sides, multiplying their reflections into infinity, so that endless rows of Svetlanas and Andreis stretched out in every direction. Even the floor was a mirror surface. The dazzle of Light was so strong that Svetlana thought the room was empty.

Then she saw a table. On the table stood a black box.

The box had a shiny body like the carapace of a beetle, several knobs and dials and a ridged grill set into its front. Svetlana had never seen anything like that. Andrei, on the other hand, peered at the thing with a dawning recognition.

"Radio?" he murmured incredulously.

The thing emitted a hoarse coughing noise, as if clearing its throat, and then a voice issued from the grill. It was a man's voice, tired and tense. It spoke with a strange accent Svetlana had never heard before.

"Report, soldier," it said.

Andrei stepped smartly forward and saluted the thing.

"Sergeant Andrei Kurchenko, Comrade Supreme Commander of the 50th Army, 17th Rifle Division, Central Front. We are holding our positions, killing fritzes day and night. No surrender, no retreat!"

"Yes," the voice said meditatively. "No surrender. My order. A bullet through your head if you are surrounded. A clean death. You have bullets, don't you, soldier?"

Andrei faltered.

"I . . . " he whispered, "I used them all up. Here. The things, the monsters. Protecting her . . . " he gestured at Svetlana who broke her paralysis and addressed the voice.

"I used up the last two bullets, Comrade Voice," she said. "To execute the traitors. It is my fault."

The voice chuckled.

"A brave girl," it said. "True daughter of Motherland! But we don't blame you. It is of no significance. Guns would not work here for long, but every bullet fired on the other side of the mirror turns into a ray of Light on this side. The more you bleed, the more we win."

"The other side of the mirror . . . " Andrei whispered. "So, this is what this is . . . I thought I was dead . . . "

"Not yet," the voice said. "But you have done a great service. You opened the door. Now we can pass through to the other side. We can fight with you. We can use your weapons for a while. The Wulfstan are doing it already, rabid dogs! They discovered the door first; this is why they have guns. But they are fools, their heads hollowed out by their mad leader, their ranks crawling with traitors! Their guns will fail and when they do, we will be so much stronger because what we take from your side is not metal but spirit. Your courage will power our factories, your purity will build our cities, your dedication will feed our workers, and your blood will be our Light."

Svetlana felt tears gathering behind her eyes. That was what she had lived for and what she now longed to die for. It made her fearless, this exaltation. Again, she addressed the Voice.

"The Enemy will be finally defeated, won't it? Our cities will be clean and well-lit. There will be no bloodsucking krovososy, no teeming kosmops, no perfidious oborotni, no greedy devouring fists. Motherland will be free."

The Voice chuckled again.

"You haven't heard me speak for a while, have you, little sister?" it said. "The war was going against us and the people were deprived of their sustenance. Now it's the time to remedy this."

And the Voice spoke.

He spoke in words of fire that meant nothing and everything; that made people forget fear and embrace hate; that made husbands abandon wives and wives turn away from husbands in pursuit of a higher love, the love of an abstraction. They made children denounce parents and call it loyalty; and parents sacrifice children and call it faith. His words swept over the pair in the hall of mirrors like the torrent of muddy floodwater in spring, destroying every shred of doubt and hesitation, washing away memories and desires, and filling the empty spaces with utter and complete devotion. The words were gibberish. They did not signify, argue, or persuade. They were what they were.

As they bounded against the surface of the mirrors that lined the room, they became flaming seeds. Instead of giving rise to miniature warriors of Light, as the Voice used to do in every home in Motherland, these seeds were doubled and trebled and infinitely multiplied by the mirrors, until Andrei and Svetlana stood in the heart of a fiery storm, flames leaping high around them, above and below. But the inferno emitted no heat. The firestorm raged but did not consume.

As the fire became too much for its own rage, it burrowed into the silver of the mirrors, breaking through the blind surfaces into what lay on the other side. The mirrors did not shatter, but instead of reflecting the black box of the Voice, they now became as transparent as windows, showing the rolling meadows, the mighty rivers, and the proud cities of Motherland. Where seeds of fire fell, they were planted, and bloomed, and bore fruit. Their fruits were the oborotni, the krovososy, the Kosmops and the Fists. The words of the Voice became the bodies of the Enemy.

GOODBYES

THEY ONLY HAD an hour or so before the train was supposed to leave. Svetlana spent much of the morning going over the med kits she had been issued before departure. There were not enough. There were three-hundred people in her combat battalion, and she only had twenty kits. But with judicious use of gauze and iodine, she could stretch it out to cover most emergencies. Well, except for those that required actual surgery. Even if she knew how to do it, there were no scalpels or sterilization supplies in the kits. There were also no doctors. Most of them were sequestered in the Health Institute right here, in the City, trying to find the cure for the black-star infestation. The last she heard, they had met with significant success. Certainly, the random Patrols that went around the City, stopping passers-by and shining an electric torch into their eyes, were finding fewer and fewer traitors. She almost never saw them execute anybody anymore. Recently, these Patrols were composed mostly of women and older men. All the men of military age were sent straight to the battlefront. In the south, select POP divisions were taking their last stand against the desperate attacks of

Wulfstan. Svetlana was not overtly concerned about those rabid dogs. She was not shy about speaking her mind, explaining to anybody who would listen—which mostly meant Maria, the old nurse responsible for coordinating and provisioning new recruits—that the supposed wonder-weapon of Wulfstan, the fire-stick, was becoming increasingly unreliable and in a short while would be rendered totally useless. Maria would shake her head, whether in agreement or negation was hard to tell because of her Parkinson's disease. Svetlana knew she was right, though.

The problem, however, was that other countries had recently joined the cowardly attack of Wulfstan on the Motherland. Dwarfish and devious Small-Landers poured over the eastern borders with their trained flying sharks. The Leech-masters sent legions of their exsanguinated subjects into the swamps of the south where their thirst for blood made them dangerous to people and livestock alike. The barbarians of Thunderland sent reinforcements to Wulfstan, for all that the latter's haughty people despised their tribal ways. Worst of all, the Enemy within was as tireless and prolific as ever, undermining the people's war efforts at every turn.

Svetlana was not worried. She knew that the leadership of the Voice would prevail and that he would deliver his people from Darkness into Light. That was all that mattered. Her own life was a small and insignificant spark to add to his fire.

Andrei waited for her outside the medical barrack as she slipped out, trying to avoid the gimlet eyes of Lyda, another trainee nurse and an inveterate gossip. Lyda was convinced that Andrei was Svetlana's boyfriend, and no matter how much she pooh-poohed the idea, Lyda would not stop her teasing. At first, Svetlana was so indignant that she complained to Maria but seeing that the latter's intervention was not likely, she resigned herself to the ribbing. What did Lyda understand anyway? Andrei was closer to her than any boyfriend could possibly be.

He stood in the dappled spring sunshine, torn clouds scudding in the warm wind. He had gained a portion of the weight he had lost during their sojourn in the Wastelands and no longer looked so gaunt. He was wearing a new spiffy Patrol uniform.

They embraced, and he led her toward the back of the barrack. They sat on a pile of sodden planks.

"So, is your unit shipped tomorrow?" she asked, just to break the silence which was beginning to feel awkward. She could gauge Andrei's moods infallibly and now she knew he was being tense, as if preparing to tell her something and trying to find the right words. Lyda would say that this ability to read his mind would give Svetlana an advantage in their relationship. Unfortunately, Lyda did not know that Andrei was just as capable of understanding Svetlana's unspoken thoughts as she was of understanding his.

He nodded.

"I know you are going south," she prattled, "it's not such a big secret as they are making it out to be, but never mind, we are being sent east but it's only for now and they promised they would send me to the training center to upgrade my skills and after that I'll be able to choose where to go, so we'll see each other soon . . . "

"Sveta," Andrei said, so softly that she had to lean into the damp gusts to grab his words before they were snatched away by the wind. "I'm going to Kurskaya Duga."

She blinked. She knew what he was trying to say but she still tried to pretend she did not, and then it would not be real.

"Where is this? The Western front?"

"On the other side of the mirror," he said.

She was silent, and he went on, speaking half to himself.

"There was that guy in the trenches. Trofim . . . an older guy, an intellectual. They were coming for him, but he was lucky—led an attack, got a bullet in the head. Clean death. He was telling me that words cast shadows and these shadows get together and weave a world for themselves and live in it, not knowing that they are shadows of our thoughts, feelings, loves, and hates. He also said that a shadow is the body of a soul. So, every man has a sister shadow that goes with him, and lives the reflection of his life, and dies the reflection of his death . . . "

"What are you talking about?" Svetlana whispered.

Andrei finally looked her straight in the face and she saw the reflection of her own blue eyes in his dark ones. She also saw that they were exactly the same shape.

"Little sister, little sister," he said. "I had a sister named Svetlana, I told you so. Only she died, my Sveta. She died when our Dad was arrested. We lost our ration card and she died because we did not have enough to eat."

"Was he an Enemy, your Dad?"

"They said he was a traitor. The NKVD came and took him away. My Mama, she stood in line every day to bring him food. Together with other women. She would get up in the middle of the night, go there, and stand in line with all those other women. I wanted to come with her, but she said no. She was afraid that if they saw me, they would remember me and arrest me too. She wrote letters to Comrade Stalin, telling him how my Dad was a good and honest man, how much he loved our country, how he would die before betraying it . . . They took the letters. I don't know what they did with them. I knew one night they would come for me too. Then the war started."

"The war . . . " Svetlana whispered. "So, you also have a war there . . . "

"We have it because you have it, or maybe it's the other way around. Who cares? Two sides to a mirror, and a word spoken on one side becomes a monster on the other. But here you are, in the world of our shadows, and it's a bad world, a hard world. I can see that. I'm sorry for all the words we said so many times, each of them becoming an Enemy to harass you. But a man got to believe in something, and there is a war, and the Germans are worse than the NKVD . . . At least, those who come to arrest you at night are our own people. There is bad and worse, and when it happens, there is no choice."

"I don't understand," Svetlana cried.

"Yes, you do."

She looked away but the running shadows of the clouds on the wet ground were like the negative of the words of fire that sowed hatred all over Motherland. She had seen it; she could not unsee.

"You also have a choice," he said, almost inaudibly. "Your parents . . . they took the black stars. They agreed. The infection only takes you over if you let it."

"No!" she cried and lifted her hand to slap him, stop his lying mouth, and let it drop.

"Would you take it?" he insisted. "Knowing what we saw in the Tower?"

"No," she said quietly. He was right. There was no choice.

"How would you do it?" she asked after a timeless interval as they huddled together in the medley of sun and shadow.

He showed her a sliver of mirror.

"I think I got shell-shocked there. I remember there was an explosion, a stray grenade maybe. I think I'm coming out of it. Last night, I dreamed, and it was . . . like I was back there again, with all the guys, and Pyotr, smoking. Ivan reading a letter from home . . . Anyway, I think if I look into the mirror just as I am falling asleep, I'll wake up there."

Svetlana nodded. There was nothing else to say and so they embraced one last time and she went to the barrack without looking back. Lyda would want to know how the date went, and she would have to make up something, tell some tall tale about the first kiss.

Except, does it count when the lips that touch yours are a shadow of your own?

SHADOWS

"Your son, unit commander Senior Sergeant Kurchenko Andrei Andreevich was wounded in the battle for the socialist Motherland. He was loyal to his military oath and showed heroism and bravery. He died of his wounds and was buried in the county cemetery of Helmsted near Magdeburg (Germany) on March 15, 1945. This letter serves as the official document for opening a pension request's proceedings (as per Order no 220 of NKO USSR)".

***

Svetlana touched Alex' hand shyly as the two of them stood on the bank of the creek, looking down into the swift water speckled with white and pink petals. Spring came early this year, and the cherry and apple trees were already in bloom. Drowning in the billows of fragrant blossoms, Little Wells looked lovely and peaceful.

She was dispatched here after the decisive rout of

Wulfstan troops on the Western front. After the years of blood, mud, screams of the wounded and cursing of the dying, the post of a rural nurse, responsible for the new clinic opening in the village, was as close to paradise as she could imagine. Then Alex, Krasnov's cousin, came back—half of his right leg missing and his brown hair gray—but alive.

They did not talk about Krasnov. Sometimes, it seemed to Svetlana that what she had experienced in this snowbound, monster-infested village had been a bad dream. Andrei had been part of this dream, but he had receded into a haze of memory, becoming like a blurry photograph or a snatch of a familiar but elusive tune: something to feed the indefinite feeling of nostalgia that stole over her from time to time.

Not when she was with her fiancé, though. This was here and now.

She looked up from her wavering reflection in the stream, turned to Alex with a smile . . .

And a dead woman broke out of the thicket of willows and lunged at her.

Svetlana tried to defend herself, raising her arms to protect her face, but the mertvez sunk her teeth into her neck. A spray of hot blood drenched both of them. The attack happened so suddenly that Alex had been paralyzed by surprise but now he turned against the dead woman, beating her over the head with his crutch. She fell but like any other mertvez, a former person, being already dead, she was not easy to kill. Her face was reduced to bloody pulp before she subsided on the ground in an ungainly heap.

Svetlana, her hand pressed to her torn neck in a gesture she knew to be futile, recognized her killer.

Swollen and gray as she was, her eyes pecked out by birds, she was the same woman who had tried to give away her dead baby to her and Andrei.

As the blossoming trees, and the blood on the grass, and Alex' face were receding, floating away from her, she called upon Andrei, knowing he was waiting for her somewhere beyond words. Those words that ricocheted between the two sides of the mirror, giving birth to monsters and miracles. The words that bred shadows of hatred and fear but also of love.

So, every man has a sister shadow that goes with him, and lives in the reflection of his life, and dies in the reflection of his death . . .

THE END?

Not if you want to dive into more of Crystal Lake Publishing's Tales from the Darkest Depths!

Check out our amazing website and online store. https://www.crystallakepub.com

We always have great new projects and content on the website to dive into, as well as a newsletter, behind the scenes options, social media platforms, and our own dark fiction shared-world series and our very own store. If you use the IGotMyCLPBook! coupon code in the store (at the checkout), you'll get a one-time-only 50% discount on your first eBook purchase!

Our webstore even has categories specifically for KU books, non-fiction, anthologies, and of course more novels and novellas.

ABOUT THE AUTHOR

Born in a country that no longer exists, Elana Gomel is an academic with a long list of books and articles, specializing in science fiction, Victorian literature, and serial killers. She is also a fiction writer who has published more than ninety short stories, several novellas, and three novels: *A Tale of Three Cities* (2013), *The Hungry Ones* (2018) and *The Cryptids* (2019). Her story "Where the Streets Have No Name" was the winner of the 2020 Gravity Award, and her story "Mine Seven" is included in The Best Horror of the Year 13 edited by Ellen Datlow

She is a member of HWA.

Her website is:
https://www.citiesoflightanddarkness.com/

She can also be found on social media:

Facebook https://www.facebook.com/elana.gomel
Twitter https://twitter.com/ElanaGomel
Instagram https://www.instagram.com/elanagomel/

Readers . . .

Thank you for reading *Little Sister*. We hope you enjoyed this novella.

If you have a moment, please review *Little Sister* at the store where you bought it.

Help other readers by telling them why you enjoyed this book. No need to write an in-depth discussion. Even a single sentence will be greatly appreciated. Reviews go a long way to helping a book sell, and is great for an author's career. It'll also help us to continue publishing quality books. You can also share a photo of yourself holding this book with the hashtag #IGotMyCLPBook!

Thank you again for taking the time to journey with Crystal Lake Publishing.

Visit our Linktree page for a list of our social media platforms. https://linktr.ee/CrystalLakePublishing

Our Mission Statement:

Since its founding in August 2012, Crystal Lake Publishing has quickly become one of the world's leading publishers of Dark Fiction and Horror books in print, eBook, and audio formats.

While we strive to present only the highest quality fiction and entertainment, we also endeavour to support authors along their writing journey. We offer our time and experience in non-fiction projects, as well as author mentoring and services, at competitive prices.

With several Bram Stoker Award wins and many other wins and nominations (including the HWA's Specialty Press Award), Crystal Lake Publishing puts integrity, honor, and respect at the forefront of our publishing operations.

We strive for each book and outreach program we spearhead to not only entertain and touch or comment on issues that affect our readers, but also to strengthen and support the Dark Fiction field and its authors.

Not only do we find and publish authors we believe are destined for greatness, but we strive to work with men and woman who endeavour to be decent human beings who care more for others than themselves, while still being hard working, driven, and passionate artists and storytellers.

Crystal Lake Publishing is and will always be a beacon of what passion and dedication, combined with overwhelming teamwork and respect, can accomplish. We endeavour to know each and every one of our readers, while building personal relationships with our authors, reviewers, bloggers, podcasters, bookstores, and libraries.

We will be as trustworthy, forthright, and transparent as any business can be, while also keeping most of the headaches away from our authors, since it's our job to solve the problems so they can stay in a creative mind. Which of course also means paying our authors.

We do not just publish books, we present to you worlds within your world, doors within your mind, from talented authors who sacrifice so much for a moment of your time.

There are some amazing small presses out there, and through collaboration and open forums we will continue to support other presses in the goal of helping authors and showing the world what quality small presses are capable of accomplishing. No one wins when a small press goes down, so we will always be there to support hardworking, legitimate presses and their authors. We don't see Crystal Lake as the best press out there, but we will always strive to be the best, strive to be the most interactive and grateful, and even blessed press around. No matter what happens over time, we will also take our mission very seriously while appreciating where we are and enjoying the journey.

What do we offer our authors that they can't do for themselves through self-publishing?

We are big supporters of self-publishing (especially hybrid publishing), if done with care, patience, and planning. However, not every author has the time or inclination to do market research, advertise, and set up book launch strategies. Although a lot of authors are successful in doing it all, strong small presses will always be there for the authors who just want to do what they do best: write.

What we offer is experience, industry knowledge, contacts and trust built up over years. And due to our strong brand and trusting fanbase, every Crystal Lake Publishing book comes with weight of respect. In time our fans begin to trust our judgment and will try a new author purely based on our support of said author.

With each launch we strive to fine-tune our approach, learn from our mistakes, and increase our reach. We continue to assure our authors that we're here for them and that we'll carry the weight of the launch and dealing with third parties while they focus on their strengths—be it writing, interviews, blogs, signings, etc.

We also offer several mentoring packages to

authors that include knowledge and skills they can use in both traditional and self-publishing endeavours.

We look forward to launching many new careers.

This is what we believe in. What we stand for. This will be our legacy.

Welcome to Crystal Lake Publishing— Tales from the Darkest Depths.